ALSO BY THE AUTHOR

THE GECKO'S GATE SERIES

The Gecko's Gate

The Gecko's Gate: Assassins

The Gecko's Gate: The Empress

The Scrapbook Quests

The Magic Cat

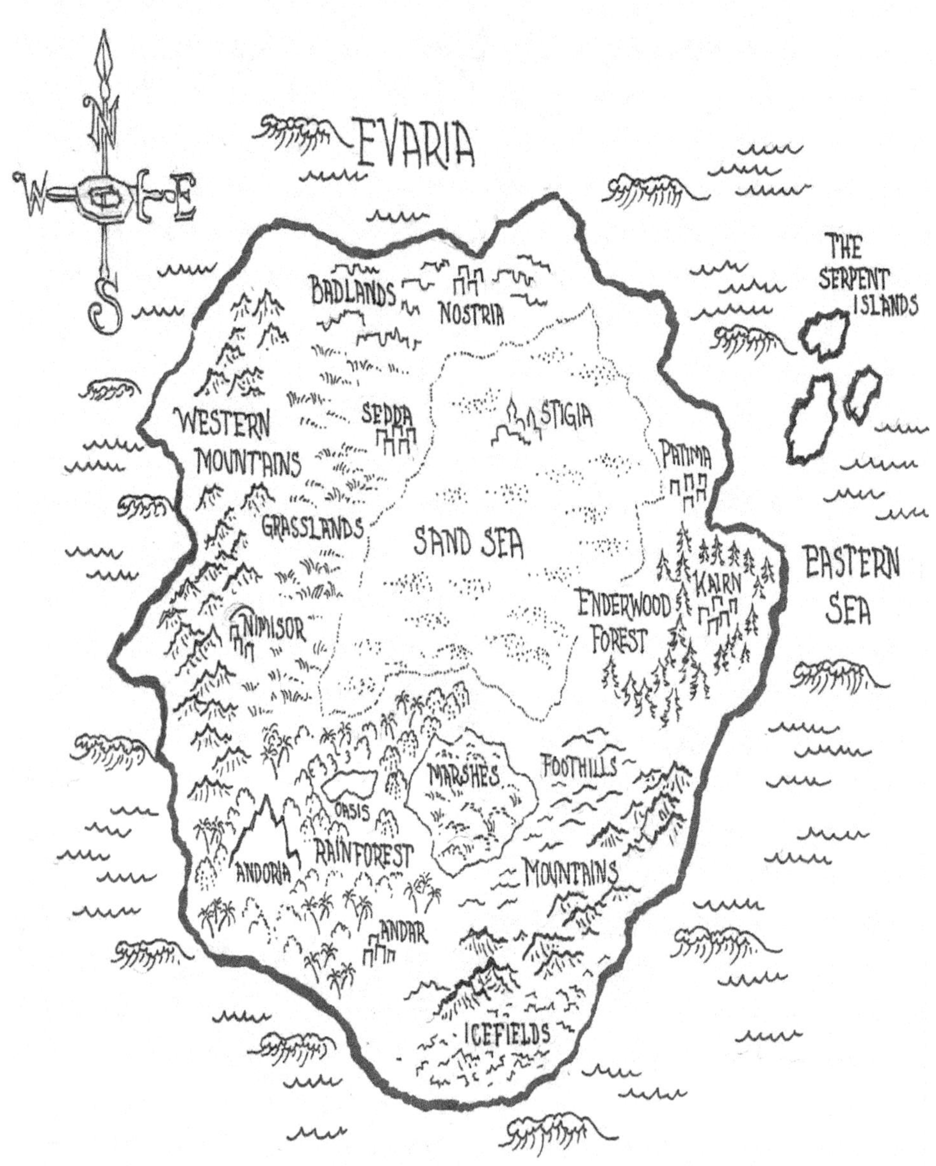

EVARIA
N
W E
S
THE SERPENT ISLANDS
BADLANDS
NOSTRIA
WESTERN MOUNTAINS
SEDDA
STIGIA
PATIMA
GRASSLANDS
SAND SEA
EASTERN SEA
NIMILSOR
ENDERWOOD FOREST
KAIRN
OASIS
MARSHES
FOOTHILLS
ANDORIA
RAINFOREST
MOUNTAINS
ANDAR
ICEFIELDS

THE GECKOS GATE
THE EMPRESS

---

sands press

THE GECKOS GATE
THE EMPRESS

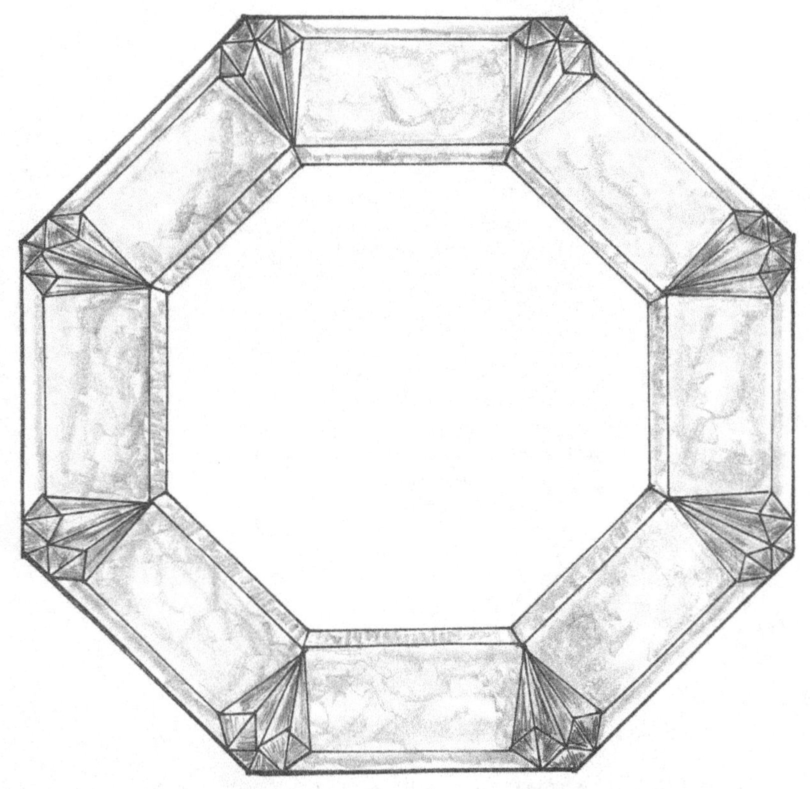

DENNIS STEIN

sands press

sands press

A division of 10361976 Canada Inc.
300 Central Avenue West
Brockville, Ontario
K6V 5V2

Toll Free 1-800-563-0911 or 613-345-2687
http://www.sandspress.com

ISBN 978-1-988281-45-2

Cover Concept by Kristine Barker and Wendy Treverton
Artwork by John Tkachuk
Gate Artwork by Sharon Stein
Edited by Alyssa Owen
Formatting by Renee Hare
Publisher Kristine Barker

Publisher's Note

For information on bulk purchases of this book or any book published by Sands Press, please call 1-800-563-0911.

1st Printing March 2018

To book an author for your live event, please call: 1-800-563-0911

Sands Press is a literary publisher interested in new and established authors wishing to develop and market their product. For more information please visit our website at www.sandspress.com.

For Kevin Davidson…

*A gentleman of amazing strength… One who managed to fight off death just
long enough to marry the love of his life.*

PART 1: THE YOUNG

Rasta knew he had to stop for a moment's rest, even though they were being followed. The gecko sat down heavily on a rock, exhausted, his legs needing a break in the dark waters of the marsh. His cape was tattered, and he rested his scaled face in his hands, wondering what they should do next. His breathing eventually slowed. For two days and nights, the Stigian troops had pursued him and the scattered remnants of his forces. They had been relentless, remaining close behind as if driven on by whips from their commanders. Rasta's soldiers were just about spent. But they had fought their way forward toward the rainforests, trying to put some distance between them and the legion of unseen Stigian soldiers. Slogging through the marsh had only tired the geckos and remaining chameleon archers further. It dragged them down, weighing down their very soul as they fought to stay ahead of the evil which was constantly at their heels.

He was from the gecko village of Andar deep in the rainforest to the south. His yellow and black scales stood out from beneath his silver armour, and he leaned heavily on his sword, trying to catch his breath in the heavy mists of the marshes. He had commanded a great column of gecko and chameleon soldiers, most having died or been wounded badly in battle. The few who struggled on through the swampy waters with him were the last remnants of what had been a large brigade of anoles, geckos, and chameleons from the rainforests, bent on curbing the Emperor of Stigia's attacks.

They had taken the battle to the very gates of Stigia itself, weary of the oppression of the Emperor of the desert kingdom. The siege had ultimately failed, however, cutting Rasta's forces to pieces, and scattering them in a charge by the horned legions pouring out of the desert city of Stigia.

He was beyond exhausted, fighting to remain upright as he glanced around at the few geckos and chameleons that struggled through the stagnant waters of the marshes. He had failed. Not only had he failed them, but he had also failed himself. Despite the aches and pains, the wounds he had suffered in battle, the worst was the idea of those reptiles who had lost their lives. They would have to return to Andar without a victory, if they made it back at all. Rasta knew that the horned legions were closing on them as they slogged through the marshes. He wanted to get through this swampy, stagnant mess before their wounds became infected, or they were too fatigued to remain ahead of the Stigian soldiers.

There was much yet to fight for, and he had to get the meagre remnants of his troops back to regroup with re-enforcements of the chameleons of Andoria. The new Chameleon King was about to be crowned, and this would raise the morale of the entire realm that fought against the tyranny of the Emperor of Stigia.

As he sat there in the bog, the tired and wounded reptile survivors of his Militia struggled through the dark waters of the marshes, a lead-grey fog surrounding them.

A lone gecko approached him, clutching his side through a split in his armour, using his sword to support him. He took a moment as he stopped in front of Rasta to catch his breath.

"My Lord, I have seen the first few groups of Stigian soldiers, entering the edge of the swamps behind us!" he gasped.

Rasta's expression dropped at this report. He had hoped that they would not be followed all the way. There was no way that his tattered band of lizards could handle another battle with the stygian horde. The gecko stood up, wincing in pain. He tore another strip of his tunic from under his armour, wrapping it around a bleeding wound on his leg.

"Have the remaining archers set themselves up on the banks of the marshes as we emerge at the edge of the forest. The Stigians will be mired in the swamp, and make themselves easier targets."

The other gecko nodded.

"At once, My Lord."

Rasta exhaled in exasperation at his words.

"And for the last time, stop calling me 'Lord', or 'Sir'! I am just another gecko, like yourself!" he exclaimed with a slight grin.

The gecko nodded again, moving off as quickly as possible to arrange his leader's plan. Rasta scanned the area around him, looking for any stragglers as he silently acknowledged the shouts of Stigian soldiers not far behind them. Without waiting any longer, he slogged forward, again aware of the pain in his leg.

The dark waters seemed to pull at him, and the mist was thick all around. At least it hid them from sight, he thought, not wanting to think about what would happen if the Stigian archers could plainly see them. Rasta kept moving, pushing aside tall green bulrushes and grasses saturated with the stagnant waters. He knew that speed was essential, getting back to the chameleon kingdom of Andoria would allow him to get re-enforcements, and get reports of battles which were happening elsewhere in the realm. Nimisor was apparently under attack, its citadel cradled in the Mountains to the west, and the treetop village of the Anoles had been set ablaze by another force of soldiers from the Stigian Empire. Few had survived.

Rasta wished it was over. He was tired. Tired of battling the endless legions of horned lizards from the desert, tired of seeing his fellow geckos killed in bloody conflicts, tired of the ceaseless assaults from Stigia on the places he loved. Some days he had desperately wanted to go back in time to be a hatchling again. No responsibilities, no war. But he was not a hatchling, and as a matter of fact, the other reptiles around him had forced him into a position within the militia of leadership, a place he was not sure he was qualified for, to say nothing about whether or not he wanted the spot.

His thoughts were interrupted as he reached the embankment of the marsh, where two dozen gecko archers peered out warily from behind a pile of boulders in the mists. Rasta sheathed his sword, climbing quickly in amongst them. He turned, looking back into the waters he had just left, the ripples caused by his passing already beginning to dissipate.

The voices of the Stigians, speaking in their own strange guttural language, emanated from the fog, the distant splashing of the tea-coloured waters growing slowly but surely louder. The gecko raised an arm silently, motioning to the archers around him. Bowstrings creaked as they tightened, pulling back on their arrows.

Rasta would make them sorry that they had chosen to pursue his remaining forces. They would pay dearly for daring to venture this close to the rainforests, he and the other lizards called home. Oh yes, they would pay…

~~~~~

The anole worked diligently, polishing a new glass bowl while tending the fire in the furnace. He was stout, but not fat, and somewhat shorter than many of the other reptiles in Andar. He had built the glassworks here in the village after he and his wife had fled the destruction of their own home high in the forest canopy. Soldiers from Stigia had set the treetop village ablaze, destroying
~~~~~

it, and killing many of their kin. The survivors had arrived here in Andar as refugees and had been welcomed warmly by the geckos who inhabited the small settlement deep in the rainforest.

His name was Binto, and he toiled here daily, sometimes with several other anoles assisting him in making beautiful wares of glass. Today was quiet, however, it was a grey and rainy day in the jungle, and he was alone in the shop. He continued to busy himself with polishing his creation to perfection, examining it periodically with a skilled eye. Once in a while he put a few pumps of air into the furnace with a bellows, keeping it hot and ready to make more glass. As he decided he was finally finished with the bowl, he strode across the room, placing it carefully on a shelf with many other works. He handled it delicately, just as he would hold his hatchling baby daughter. Binto's wife Marise had lain the egg months before, and it had sat in a small basket in the spare room of their small home, warm and awaiting the day when it would hatch. One of the village elders had determined that the couple would have a girl hatchling, by carefully examining the egg in front of a candle. Neither of the two anoles were really concerned whether their new arrival would be a boy or girl, they were simply happy that the embryo inside the egg was in perfect health. It had only hatched a few weeks before, and the new parents were kept very busy chasing the newborn girl around.

Binto took a break, sitting on a stool by the open doorway. A light rain fell as he gazed out from the covered porch to the cobblestone street and the village square beyond. He had always found the sound of the rain soothing, and it had helped when he missed their old home high in the jungle canopy.

Marise appeared, walking swiftly with a cloth bag in one scaled hand, and the bundled hatchling in the other arm. She had brought Binto some lunch of dried beetles and some nectar to drink. The male anole smiled, getting up from his stool and ushering his wife inside and out of the rain. He took the lunch bag, replacing it with a clean rag so that she could dry her scales.

The female anole began to tell him about the morning, detailing each and every thing that their young female hatchling had done so far. Binto listened intently as he munched away, smiling broadly at the stories of his daughters adventures. He always enjoyed his wife's updates and considered his small family to be very lucky to be able to spend as much time as they did together. He considered it a blessing to see his anole wife and daughter each day, even while he worked in the small shop near the village square. Today the stillness in the rainforest air, and the heavy falling rain seemed a perfect backdrop over their discussion about the tiny hatchling. It was quiet and comfortable and Binto remained riveted to Marise's words.

Such was lunchtime at the glassworks for Binto and his wife most days. They enjoyed the peace here in Andar, even if the Empire of Stigia threatened other distant settlements from their desert city. The shadow of war had hung like a black cloud over the realm for several years, as the Emperor of Stigia sent his warlords and troops throughout the lands of Evaria. He sought to expand his control of the realm, and to either enslave or destroy the other races of the world. Even in Andar, many of the male reptile inhabitants had left to join forces with their chameleon friends from the nearby caverns of Andoria, in a bid to defend their rainforest homes from the threat posed by the Stigian troops. Binto himself had transformed the glassworks into a forge to make weapons for the troops who would fight against the oppression of the Empire from the Sand Sea. He remembered the endless days of exhausting work, in extreme heat from the furnace. It was definitely not like creating the beauty of glass, instead forging swords and spears dedicated to killing. As an artisan, it hurt his very soul. He knew, however, that had he not invested the time and effort, that Stigia would run over the rest of the realm roughshod. And so, he had toiled tirelessly, experimenting with the dark and hard metals, nothing like the artwork he really enjoyed.

Today was nothing like that. He was back to creating breathtaking works in glass, enjoying lunch with his wife and newly born hatchling daughter.

"Our little one is learning very quickly!" said Marise with a smile, "Just this morning she stood up on her own!"

A broad smile came across Binto's scaled face once again as he looked down at his bundled up young daughter, who had decided it was time for a nap.

"She is simply amazing, isn't she?" asked Binto simply.

He ate another beetle, washing it down with a gulp of nectar, his eyes never leaving her. Ever since she had hatched, Binto had been fascinated by everything she did, every movement she made. He and his wife had always wanted a child of their own, and after settling in Andar, had decided it was time.

Binto rose from his chair silently so as not to awaken his daughter, still sleeping peacefully in her mother's scaled arms. He went to the furnace, giving it a blast of air as quietly as possible to keep the coals red hot. He strode slowly back toward the chair where Marise still sat. She turned her smiling gaze upward to him.

He was thoughtful for a few moments, as he looked at the two of them, listening to the spattering of rain outside in the jungle. He wished that time would stop, so that this peaceful moment would not slip away, lost in the forward march of the cosmos around them.

Marise could see the reflection of his thoughts in his eyes.

"What is it, my dear?" she asked, still smiling.

His gaze was warm as he looked down at his daughter once again.

"You and little Kiko are the two best things in my life..." he said quietly.

~~~~~

To a young gecko like Alibesh, the passing scenery was boring. She sat in the back of a covered wagon, one of several in the caravan. It bumped along the path out of the rainforest, where it met the shorter palmetto groves bordering the desert. For what seemed like forever, the caravan had been moving through the scrub bushes toward the east, on their way to a distant village to trade their spices and glassware for other goods that were needed in Andar.

The young gecko looked out the back of the wagon her parents were driving, the vehicles being pulled along the sandy trail by large turtles. The journey was not exactly speedy, but it was steady, the shelled beasts never seeming to tire, lumbering forth without complaint.

The wagon was very simple, made of dark wood from the jungle, and covered in a thin, light coloured fabric to shield the occupants and cargo from the blasting sun. It rocked and creaked along the rough road through the palmetto, and Alibesh watched the world go by, lost in thoughts of grand adventures to pass the time.

She had heard the adults talk, heard the quiet conversations about the Great Wars and the Stigian Empire. There were hushed arguments between her mother and father about the conflict in the realm. Her father had decided that soon, he must join the others in Andar who were organizing a militia to assist in the battles alongside the neighbouring kingdom. Alibesh's mother was obviously against any idea of him leaving them alone, not wishing to see Horned soldiers from Stigia attack the rainforest villages without him being there to protect them.

She was still very young, having not even molted once yet. She continued to watch the scenery pass outside the fabric covering of the wagon, clutching a small wooden carving of a snail. It was her favourite. She knew that there
~~~~~

were bad reptiles out in the big world she was looking out at, but all she could do was trust that her mother and father would keep her safe. It was not much to ask for a young gecko. Life had been peaceful, despite the tension that she sometimes heard in her parent's voices, when they thought she was not listening, or asleep. But Alibesh was always paying attention to everything around her. She was usually very quiet, a situation which had concerned her gecko parents at one time. Eventually, they just decided that their daughter didn't have much to say, and it had not dissuaded her from smiling or playing. She simply didn't speak a lot.

The wagon hit a hole in the makeshift road on one side, and Alibesh was forced to react quickly to keep her balance. Her thoughts returned to the present, as she moved closer to the opening in the fabric covering, to see more of what was outside.

It was late morning, and the sun was high above the palmetto. The temperature had risen quickly, and the air was drier, a clear indication that the caravan was skirting the edge of the desert. Cicadas emitted their high-pitched songs in the shade of the palmettos. The heat had awakened them, the male insects sensing the need to find a mate to prevent their demise as a species.

Alibesh's senses perked up as she heard new sounds. There was a rustling in the palmettos on either side of the rough, sandy road. Her vertically slit eyes scanned the undergrowth, as she tried to pinpoint where the commotion was coming from. Unsure of what was happening, she tightened her grip on the toy wooden snail. The fanlike fronds of the palmetto shook and moved along either side of the caravan, and now Alibesh could hear her parent's voices, sounding strained and nervous suddenly.

The wagon lurched and then halted abruptly, and she lost her balance, almost flipping over backward with the force. Cries of surprise and terror erupted in her ears, and the sound of clattering steel and the swishing of the palmetto surrounded the wagon. Alibesh shuddered slightly, as the cries turned to screams of pain. Something was killing the reptiles they travelled with. It registered quickly in her brain. Even being scarcely older than a hatchling, she knew what was happening. She laid flat, looking toward the front opening of the wagon's light fabric covering, now covered with smatterings of reptilian blood. Her parents were no longer sitting on the wooden bench at the front, and Alibesh could not see where they had gone. Screams and cries continued as she remained frozen still, partly hidden from view by several toppled baskets and spice containers in the back of the wagon.

There was scuffling outside, along with more sounds of steel meeting scaly flesh. Bloodcurdling screams, and Alibesh stiffened as she heard the voice of her father pleading for mercy from an unseen attacker. Blood flew against the side of the wagon, staining the fabric cover crimson, and she heard nothing more.

Quiet returned, save for the rustling of the creatures who had assailed the once peaceful caravan. She shivered with fear, paralyzed. She dared not move a muscle as she strained to listen. Low guttural voices could be made out but were far enough away that she could not understand what was being said. Another tremor of fear rocked her scaled body as she could hear the voices come closer. The young gecko remained motionless, hoping that her parents would appear once again to make everything well. She closed her eyes, attempting to block out the sounds of the strange attackers who were coming ever closer to her hiding place.

For a moment, she withdrew into her own mind as if she had left the chaos of the present unfolding around her and went to some safe place inside. It was peaceful here, as it had always been, filled with visions of her home in Andar, amongst the huge rainforest around her. Her parents were here, comforting the young one, keeping anything bad away. There was nothing wrong here, inside her mind. She blocked out the sounds around her, going to a place where everything was good, where everything was beautiful. No one would harm her. Why had her parents left her all alone? Who were these evil creatures who had attacked them?

The female gecko was yanked back into reality as a scaled hand grabbed her arm and roughly pulled her from her hiding spot on the floor of the wagon. She was tossed out onto the ground, the wind knocked out of her, a puff of dust rising from the sand covered road. Looking up, she got her first good look at her assailants. They were not very tall, their reptilian faces and heads covered in spikes protruding from their copper coloured helmets. The spears pointed at her were copper tipped, as was the armour they wore. She had never seen reptiles like them before, they were certainly nothing like the lizards who inhabited the rainforest.

She tightened her grip on the toy snail, holding it close to her. It was all she had left. The evil looking lizards leered at her.

"We should just kill her, like the rest of the gecko scum!" said one of the horned creatures to another.

"No. She might fetch us a nice reward as a slave in Stigia!" another croaked, his eyes filled with greed.

The horrifying sight of these strange creatures was enough, and Alibesh glanced behind them at the motionless, bloodied bodies of her parents lying in the sand. Why had they not protected her from these strange reptiles? Why had they not been stronger? Even though a pang of grief gripped her, making her feel almost sick with the thoughts of being alone without them, a new emotion also became intertwined inside of her; Anger. She didn't let out a whimper or cry, but tears silently began to stream from her large eyes, wetting the scales of her face. She made a promise to herself in the quiet of her own mind. No matter what these horrid creatures did to her, no matter the unspeakable terrors that the future might hold, she would not let them see fear. She would be strong.

She did not have to worry about these creatures, or what atrocities they might commit on her, because they did the worst thing that any adult could do to a hatchling who had suddenly been orphaned. They turned and left her...

~~~~~

The hatchling had always had issues with walking, despite everything that his gecko parents had done to help him. He seemed better off sitting, or crawling. Today he sat happily splashing in a puddle while his mother and father hung the family's clothing to dry in the sunshine after its wash in the nearby stream. It had rained earlier, and the cobblestone streets of Andar were just beginning to dry up now that the sun had emerged. It was a perfect spot for Jonas to be occupied for a few minutes, while his parents toiled at necessary jobs.

Water had always been a good distraction for the young gecko, the sight of which would cause him to drop whatever he might be doing to investigate it. This had sometimes been an issue, especially when his father was trying to concentrate on fishing in the nearby stream for dinner, and Jonas had ventured too close to the clear waters. In he had gone, a small splash alerting his father to trouble. After getting the coughing, sputtering hatchling back onto dry land, his parents had quickly decided that Dad would sneak off to fish alone the next time.

Jonas happily slapped at the water in the puddle, making a few excited sounds. He was able to say very few words yet, but was in perfect health for a young gecko, which was all his parents were really concerned with at the time. His appetite was good, and except for his balance issues when walking sometimes, he was a perfectly normal hatchling.
~~~~~

His mother smiled as she turned her attention to what he was doing for a moment. She thought about how much peace they had enjoyed in Andar in recent years. It was nice that she and her husband, geckos both hatched and raised in the rainforest, could enjoy such peace and tranquility, finally able to raise a hatchling of their own. It made their lives complete in a way, settled and contented. Life had become less about worrying about the Stigian hordes attacking them yet again during the time of the Great War, to warm, humid evenings where they went for a walk around the village at dusk, watching the fireflies light up the forests, and perhaps stopping at the Great Hall for one of the village elder's stories by the fireplace.

Jonas splashed in the puddle again, giggling to himself suddenly. His father turned around now, finished with hanging up the last of their woven tunics. He stepped closer to his wife, wrapping a scaled arm around her as they watched Jonas play happily. Smiles lit their faces.

The bright light of the sun through the canopy of the rainforest faded now, and Jonas' father gazed upwards through the greenery high above. Birds still sang their songs, and the sound of insects had intensified. Rains were coming again. It was nothing unusual, it was expected during the monsoon season as a matter of fact. He motioned to his wife, and the line of clothing they had just finished hanging. She rolled her eyes and slumped her shoulders, still with a slight smile. They would have to bring the still damp clothing inside, lest they had to start all over again with the laundry.

The rain could already be heard tapping on the leaves high above as the first rumble of thunder rolled across the skies. Jonas reached upward, laughing lightly as the odd droplet of cool water penetrated the thick growth of the jungle. His mother gathered the sopping wet youngster up in her arms as her husband scrambled to get their clothing back into a large woven basket from the line. Jonas struggled a little at first, still wanting to play.

Soon the leaves became weighed down with the rains, and more and more water fell through the canopy of the rainforest, pelting the undergrowth and the village buildings below. Jonas' parents moved quickly to gather the last of the clothing, giggling just as loudly as the hatchling at the sudden rainstorm. It felt cool and refreshing, a nice break from the stifling heat and humidity of the jungle.

Having finished with the clothes, they sprinted for their simple house, made of large stones with a thatched roof. It was the same as most of the other buildings in Andar, a small but comfortable dwelling perfectly suited to the young gecko family. Jonas' mother moved quickly in the stone entryway of the house with the hatchling in one arm, her husband close behind. He lugged the basket of clothing inside, breathing heavily.

They turned back to the doorway again, as the rain began to really pour, thunder once again crashing overhead.

The two geckos looked at one another, with a sigh and a smile.

"Looks like we might have to hang the laundry up inside!" Jonas' mother exclaimed.

Her husband simply shrugged, his gaze falling on his hatchling son. Jonas was mesmerized by the falling rain outside the stone entrance to the house, his eyes wide and lost in the moment.

"He will have lots of water puddles to play in when this is over..." he said.

~~~~~

The large fireplace in the Great Hall in Andar crackled and flickered in the dying light of evening as Lanwyn finally took a seat in his comfortable chair by the hearth. As the elder sat down in the wooden rocker, it was difficult for anyone nearby to tell which creaked more; the wood or his aging bones.

Many of the young reptiles from Andar sat on the warm stone floor in front of Lanwyn, geckos and anoles, males and females, waiting patiently for the gecko elder to begin one of his fascinating stories in front of the fireplace. It had become a sort of small tradition, the stories being told after a banquet or feast was held in the Great Hall, which was usually five or six times during the year. It was especially popular during the monsoon season in the rainforest, when cooler temperatures in the evening hours caused the adults and young alike to cuddle up close while listening to an epic tale by the heat of the fire.

Lanwyn had many favourite stories to tell from distant strange and wonderful places in the realm, never seeing the need to commit any of them to paper. He had told them to each new generation, and they were well memorized. He had stories of the frogs in the mountain Citadel of Nimisor, the toads from Patima who were fishermen on the Eastern Sea, strange creatures and magnificent beasts that lived in the rainforests around them, and the Sand Sea of the desert beyond. He also had stories about the oppressive Emperor, the tyrant who ruled over the horned armies of the Empire of Stigia.

It was here, in the Great Hall, where Chase's mother had brought him this particular evening, the young gecko lost immediately in the story as Lanwyn
~~~~~

began to tell a tale from long ago in a faraway land. Chase loved to hear the stories as much as any of the other reptiles gathered there. He sat with the rest of the young, lounging on the cool flagstone of the floor in the hall, listening to the fire crackle alongside the soothing tones of Lanwyn's voice.

Chase's mother smiled as she watched her son still cross-legged on the floor with the others, barely moving a muscle due to his enthrallment with the story. She sipped from a warm mug of nectar, next to one of the long banquet tables with some of the other adult geckos and anoles. With her husband off leading some of the militia that had been gathered to fight the horned legions of Stigia, she welcomed these moments of peace, where Chase's questions about where his father was and when he would be home finally abated for short periods.

Lanwyn began to really embellish the story now, and the adults grinned watching the children's eyes widen as they remained fixated on the tale. Outside, a chorus of insects began to sing in the darkening undergrowth, but here, inside the warmth of the Great Hall, the only sound was Lanwyn's voice over the crackling fire. Aromas from the large kitchen area at the back of the building wafted inviting smells as the banquet was cleaned up.

Peace and tranquility were something that each and every villager in Andar wanted right now, with the wars raging throughout the realm against the Stigian Empire. Most of the males that were of age to fight had left to join the armies fighting with the Chameleon against the horned legions from the desert kingdom. A separate conflict had erupted in the west at the foot of the mountains which cradled the Citadel of Nimisor. The frogs of Nimisor were besieged by a Stigian Warlord, who was well known for his barbaric and brutal tactics.

For now, at least, life remained calm and peaceful in the rainforest village. Chase lounged on the floor of the Great Hall with the other young geckos and anoles, caught up in a magical story under the watchful gaze of his mother.

Several of the younger ones began to yawn here and there, and Lanwyn winked at the parents sitting around one of the large tables without breaking the storyline he was continuing. The fire had begun to burn low, its embers glowing warmly in the ever-darkening hall. As the young began to drop off to sleep listening to the soothing sounds of the elder's voice, several of the adults moved to scoop up their hatchlings delicately, ready to take them back to a warm bed for the night.

Chase however, was always resilient to this story time 'sleeping potion'.

He would always stubbornly remain affixed to Lanwyn's tale until it was finished, sometimes being the only one of the young to remain, and often with questions for the elder about the tale. His mother simply shrugged with a smile at Lanwyn's amazed expression.

"What happened after that?" was the usual question from the young gecko.

"Well, we will continue the story another night!" replied Lanwyn calmly.

"But why does the story never have an ending?" Chase continued to ask.

"Time has no beginning and no end, my young friend. And So, like time, neither does the story..."

"But..."

Sensing the conversation going in circles, Lanwyn held up a hand suddenly. He still smiled at Chase apologetically, and glanced up at his mother, who looked as if she could fall asleep in her chair at this point.

"If I told you all of the story at once, young gecko, then what would I have to share with you after the next banquet?" Lanwyn asked patiently.

This abruptly stopped the line of questions momentarily as Chase became thoughtful, processing what the elder had said. His mother stifled a giggle.

It only lasted for a moment, as Chase's expression brightened, a sudden realization reaching his young mind.

"Well, time would begin all over again, in a different place!" he replied simply.

Lanwyn sat back comfortably in his chair for a moment, scratching the scales of his chin, considering the young lizard's words. They were simplified, the way that a young mind worked, but in that small sentence, the elder realized that Chase had captured a very large idea which turned the way most of the inhabitants of their world viewed time and space that enveloped them upside down. Finally, he responded.

"Give a young brain enough time to think, and all the mysteries of the universe will eventually be solved..."

Chase looked at him without anything else to say, digesting the elder's thoughts on the matter. His mother, however, finally stood up from her chair with a yawn herself.

"Let's go young one, you can solve the rest of the realm's problems another night..." she said.

~~~~~

The young chameleon stood silently, just trying to remember to breathe.
~~~~~

He had known that this day would come for some time now, but here he stood, and he was nervous. He had tried to hide it but was conscious of the other mystics watching him as they brought his cape and fussed about preparing him.

Sunlight poured in through the large opening in the high ceiling of the cavern, spilling bright light throughout the many gardens of the chameleon kingdom of Andoria. Wildflowers absorbed the warm radiance, oblivious to the festivities in the cavern that they grew in. Brightly coloured fish swam in the stream which wound through Andoria's interior, it's clear, cool waters flowing slowly through the gardens and under several ornate bridges before disappearing under the walls of rock.

This day would change many things for the young chameleon mystic. For many years he had studied and practiced, his visions and meditations raising him above a mere acolyte in the mystical arts. His father had taught him many things, and his mother had been especially adept at healing. But this day had very little to do with any of that. He had already received the blessings of his teachers and been and welcomed as a full-fledged Mystic within his order. Today his position within Andoria would change forever. After his father's unexpected passing, and a period of mourning, the young chameleon, resplendent in his father's silver armour, the red cape much too long for him, stood silently awaiting his fate. He had not yet had a final molting, and therefore had not reached his full growth. The other mystics had tried to make everything fit as best they could, as they waited for the ceremony to begin.

The chameleon exhaled deeply, attempting to look calm. Today he would take on the weight of a great deal of responsibility, not only in his own kingdom, but for the realm as a whole. Today he was to be crowned the Chameleon King.

The leaders of the other races of the world of Evaria were all present for this important event, and at the conclusion of it all, he already had to meet several of the reptile dignitaries to discuss a variety of matters of mutual concern.

He knew that his life would be like this at times going forward. Schedules, meetings, formal appointments, not to mention a great deal of additional learning about the politics among the races of Evaria. There was also diplomacy and negotiations with the horned lizards of the desert Empire of Stigia, a situation which the chameleon knew full well had not gone well in the past.

Just then, another young chameleon mystic appeared in the grove of trees that he was waiting in. It was Ubius, his dear friend and a trusted advisor at times like this.

"How are you, are you ready?" asked Ubius, observant of his friend's obvious nervousness.

"About as ready as I will ever be, I guess..." he replied, attempting a small smile.

Ubius sighed, grinning back.

"Although I love seeing you nervous for once in your life Maxxus, there is really nothing to be troubled about. You have been preparing for this day your entire life..." said Ubius.

"Well, it is a day that I was hoping would wait a while longer to arrive." Maxxus replied quietly.

After a few more last minute checks that everything was in order with his friend's appearance, Ubius disappeared for a few minutes from the grove of trees where they had been preparing Maxxus for the ceremony. The sudden absence of his friend and most trusted advisor made him feel all the more alone, and he exhaled, realizing that this would all be over with eventually. If he could get through the coronation, then things would be fine after that. There would be the shaking of hands with the leaders of the other races, most of which he already knew thanks to his father. Then the banquet, where he would make a brief speech, and a toast to all who were gathered there to celebrate,... etc, etc.

He felt a pang of remorse, knowing that his father would have given stern words to Maxxus' lack of enthusiasm. He missed his father. He had not only been a strong leader for their people, respected by all the races of Evaria, but a comfort to Maxxus, always reassuring to be near.

It wasn't that he was not excited that he was being crowned to lead Andoria, he just hated the whole ceremony thing. It would be better tomorrow when it was all over.

He could hear the conversations of gathered reptiles echoing throughout the cavern and tried to focus on the task ahead. The waiting was what he hated. He was even more anxious about meeting with the leaders of the other races. Maxxus had never felt that politics was his strong suit. And the chameleon knew very well what the topic of discussion would be; the growing aggression and hostilities from the desert kingdom of Stigia. It hung over the entire realm like a black storm cloud. The self-proclaimed 'Emperor' of Stigia had been attacking neighbouring kingdoms and villages in the attempt to bring more of Evaria under his control and rule. Several of the smaller settlements on the edges of the desert had no real military or defenses to speak of, and had to settle with occupation by the horned legions of Stigia. In a few cases, all out slavery had prevailed.

A voice from somewhere behind shook him back to the present. It was friendly and familiar to Maxxus, and a smile broke over his scaled face.

"Wow. All dressed up and nowhere to go, huh?" the voice asked jokingly.

The chameleon turned, and reached out to grasp the hand of a gecko who had emerged from the trees surrounding the grove. The two reptiles smiled broadly at one another for a moment, shaking hands.

"It is good to see you, my friend." Maxxus replied warmly.

The gecko was dressed in silver armour very similar to his own, and wore a short red cape to make his attire a little more formal. A sword hung from his side, in a polished silver scabbard.

" I hear that once these pleasantries are over with, you might be putting together an army to go and teach those horned scum a lesson!" the gecko said.

Maxxus grinned at him.

"I figured you might be just the lizard I need to lead one of our columns, Rasta." he replied. "What concerns me the most right now is the siege at Nimisor. That crazed warlord Cyrus Malthor seems to be the hammer against the anvil for the Emperor of late. I have yet to have the crown placed on my head and the representatives from the mountain citadel are out there wanting to speak with me already."

Rasta smacked the chameleon on the shoulder, still smiling.

"Well, that's what it is to be King, you know, it's not all feasting and drinking all the time!" he stated playfully.

Maxxus smiled at his friend fondly, giving him a quick wink. He knew somehow that he and this gecko had a great adventure lying ahead of them, for better or worse. He could feel that together, they just might be able to bring about a realm where the races could live together in peace, unafraid.

Several of the chameleon mystics suddenly appeared, and Maxxus knew they were to escort him to his coronation, in front of the entire kingdom. He raised a scaled hand, a silent request for another moment with his friend. He looked at Rasta seriously now, speaking in a low tone.

"I want you to have something, my friend…"

PART 2: THE EMPRESS

~20~

1

The crack of wooden swords meeting one another filled the air in the arena, the gathered reptiles, and amphibians following every movement of the two combatants as they traded blows on the sandy floor of their battleground. The tournament had attracted a large crowd of onlookers, and the event had eventually come down to this final showdown. A horned lizard from the Empire of Stigia in the Sand Sea, and a female gecko, from a village in the grasslands. The two fighters had come to represent their homelands, and to win glory for their people.

Those watching shouted and cheered as the two lizards attacked and countered each other's attacks. They danced around and toward one another, locked in combat. Sand flew as they lunged at each other, drawing more attention from the watching crowd. The horned Stigian attacked, only to be blocked by the quick moves of the female gecko. She countered, turning quickly and sweeping a scaled leg under her assailant, knocking him down. She moved in for the kill, but her enemy deflected her wooden sword, its dull point slamming harmlessly into the sand of the arena floor. The horned lizard rolled quickly away from her, able to once again spring back to his feet. The two fighters squared off again, pausing with swords at the ready to plan their next moves.

The crowd continued to shout, encouraging the two to continue. They were drunk on the excitement of the arena, and beer made from nectar. Alibesh and the Stigian were both breathing heavily now, but showed each other no signs of fatigue.

"You cannot beat me, little gecko!" sneered the Stigian.

Alibesh did not dignify his statement with any response. She shifted her leather armour, and raised her wooden sword into the high guard, changing her footing as if to dare him to attack her. A taunt. It did not go unnoticed, and the crowd came alive, jeering and yelling at the Horned Stigian to attack the female gecko. He snarled with irritation, lunging forward at her, thrusting his sword in a vicious attack.

For Alibesh, time seemed to slow as her enemy moved toward her, and she could see several moves ahead of him, his charge at her was unbalanced, probably due to his sudden anger with her taunting him. He had proven easy to trick. Now he attacked carelessly. Her eyes narrowed as he came toward her, swinging downward onto his outstretched weapon. Instead of trying to dodge him, she quickly grabbed his scaled arm with her free hand, pulling him directly toward her. His forward momentum only made him fall forward toward her side. Alibesh raised her arm horizontally and lunged into the Stigian's path as hard as possible, her arm catching him directly at neck level.

The force of the impact sent the rest of the horned lizards lower body forward, flipping him over so hard with the clothesline effect she had lined up, that he landed on his neck and shoulders. A loud crunch could be heard as he impacted the sand of the arena floor, and his body crumpled into the dirt, motionless.

The crowd went crazy, cheering and shouting in a thunderous calamity. Alibesh stood firmly, not looking at her fallen opponent, or concerned about him getting back up to continue the fight. It was over. The gecko did not have to check on her enemy to know that he would not be getting up from where he laid in the sand. He was dead, and everyone knew it. She stared at the crowd without emotion, even as they roared in approval. As the noise of the arena continued, Alibesh walked out of the sand and into the shade of her tent, which was set up on the outer edge of the arena, already slinging her sword away. There would be no more battles today. She had defeated all of her enemies once again, but this last fight had shown a bit of finality. It was not supposed to be a fight to the death. It was the reason that the combatants used wooden weapons instead of steel. But when a reptile stepped into the arena to fight, they were all well aware of the reality of their occupation. Still, Alibesh was sure that the group from Stigia would not be very happy about what she had done to their fighter.

As if in answer, two reptiles stepped into the tent, skinks who were her trainers. They were a long way from the grasslands they called home. Alibesh let a grin creep onto her scaled face.

"I know you are pleased with yourself, but perhaps you should refrain from killing your opponents?" said one of the skinks.

"I am sure that bets were won…" Alibesh replied quietly, the rush of the fight beginning to finally subside.

"It might be wise to restrain your tactics just slightly when facing a fighter from Stigia…" said the other skink, levelling his gaze at her with a serious tone.

She simply smiled at them, and without another word, she sat on a small stool in the corner of the tent, reaching for some dried insects and a flask of nectar from a nearby table. She rested a moment, conscious of the looks she was getting from the two skinks watching her. Peeling at the buckles of her leather armour, she stripped it off, ignoring the fact that her trainers averted their eyes as she reached for a soft tunic to throw on instead. She had never been one to worry too much about modesty. She was very beautiful as far as geckos were concerned, and she knew it as well.

"It is not my fault that the others who fight against me are inferior. I was trained by *you*, to be the best, to be victorious at all costs." she said, pointing up at them.

"Yes, but that does not mean you should enter the arena with a wooden sword and still KILL the warriors who have been sent by the other races, especially when it concerns Stigia!" exclaimed one of the skinks, raising his arms toward the ceiling of the tent for added emphasis.

The other skink nodded in agreement. This would definitely not be taken lightly by the horned ones of the desert. They would not like being made to look weak or stupid.

"I think it would be wise for us to depart for Sedda as soon as possible. I think that the Stigians will be very angry with this. The loss of money is one thing, but it is the embarrassment to them that concerns me." he said.

This did not seem to change Alibesh's expression, and she simply waved a scaled hand at them in frustration, continuing to munch and drink. Seeing their exasperated looks at her apparent lack of concern, she finally flung the remaining pieces of food to the sand floor inside the tent, setting the flask back onto the table firmly. She stood up defiantly, placing scaled hands on her hips, and giving the two reptiles a look that lacked both patience and emotion.

"Please Alibesh, we are on dangerous ground here. This will not be looked on well for us or for you…" the first skink said pleadingly.

She sighed, tired of the discussion. She toyed with her soft tunic, doing a slight twirl for them, but picking up her wooden sword as she did so and pointing it in their direction.

"I am what you taught me to be." she replied simply.

~~~~~
~~~~~

The jungle canopy allowed little light in, the undergrowth draped in shadow. On the forest floor, as twilight fell, the glow of mushrooms mixed with the bio-luminescence of certain large ferns bathed the ground in hues of blue and green light. No torchlight was necessary in this corner of the rainforest, for the living light of the plants here came alive in the evening hours, and through the night. It was a place where the jungle had evolved to light the darkness, where all of the life in the forest basked in the strange glow of the plants which grew here.

The warm air was saturated by humidity, heavy and still as the night sound of insects filled the space. A slight mist hung above the ground in this remote part of the rainforest, as the ferns and mushrooms cast their glow in the gathering darkness, illuminating the jungle from below. The taller ferns served as living lamps, glowing green as night fell.

A path led through the luminous undergrowth, covered in mosses which also shed a dim green glow, as it led up to higher ground. In the middle of this vast, lit area of the rainforest, a large rocky outcrop rose. Ancient rock, hard and grey amidst the soft mosses and fauna which surrounded it.

Small bronze pools of liquid metal dotted the surface of the outcrop, numbering many, lying in shallow holes carved in the rock over the millennia. The glow of the plants of this huge grove shone off the bright metal ponds, their contents a concealed secret.

In this small corner of Evaria, in the most remote of places in the rainforest, the glowing grove was undisturbed, a place of mystery. Few of the reptile inhabitants of the realm had ever seen the glow of the undergrowth at night, illuminating the jungle in the twilight hours. It had remained pristine for millennia, as the plants had evolved over time to become luminescent. This sacred place had emerged as a place of sanctuary, where few had visited. There were stories of it, buried in years of tales told by firelight, where even the elders among the races of reptiles knew only what had been passed down to them. In the end, very little was known about the glowing grove, and the secrets it held. Only the mystics amongst the chameleons of Andoria knew anything about this place. They had harvested select pieces of the fauna, using them to light their pathways, and sharing the glowing mushrooms with the other races of the rainforest. The same blue glowing mushrooms lined the streets of the gecko village of Andar, a gift from the chameleon kingdom. It was a place of great peace and beauty, where all of the creatures of the jungle flourished.

Day in and day out, the mist and the rain nurtured the grove, appearing normal during the daylight hours, and transforming into a natural glowing gallery at night. The plants of the grove illuminated the jungle around them during the darkness, as if each piece of living plant life was a light in the night. There was no need for a torch here.

The secrets held by the glowing grove would remain a mystery, despite the prophecy of *The Three*, until new eyes beheld the strange glow of the undergrowth at night. The pools of bronze liquid bubbled on the rock outcrop within the grove, unwilling to give up their secrets. To stare into them was to give up the observer's soul, mesmerized by the metallic liquid within the pools in the rock. So was the story that had been told about the grove by the few who knew it.

The ancient races of Evaria had held on to a belief that a weapon of great power had been hidden in the Glowing Grove, within the very same pools in the rock. Where this weapon had come from, or the details of its origin were long lost, except in tales from before the recorded history of the realm. But there still remained a few reptiles who knew the legends. Whether or not this weapon actually existed had become myth and legend, a story seldom told amongst the races of Evaria. It was rumoured that a sword of immense power had been placed there, beyond the reach of any reptile that did not have the mark upon them. A mark which would allow them to retrieve the sword when the time came, when that chosen individual would help to once again bring lasting peace to the realm…

This story had not been written on any parchment or scroll, but instead handed down in stories told to the young. There were very few who actually knew the tale, most having dismissed it as fantasy, or forgotten it long ago. There was no reptile alive that could confirm or deny this ancient story, and only a limited number who would dare speak of it aloud.

The grove continued to glow in shades of blues and greens, purples and reds throughout each night, the plants carrying on their silent vigil. If a sword or other weapon was hidden here, it was well protected from the outside world, and with few of the realm's creatures knowing anything about it, the grove would not likely give up its secrets easily.

~~~~~

Chase moved slowly through the rainforest, his eyes keen for any movement. He was low in the undergrowth, his spear at the ready. He turned his head slightly and caught Jonas' silhouette in the corner of his vision,
~~~~~

several steps behind. They had already managed to spear many large beetles, filling their packs with the harvest. The two geckos worked well together, hunting as one.

The smell of the jungle filled his senses, and the fresh oxygen emitted by the greenery-filled his breath as he crept forward. The sounds of the rainforest were all around, birds in the canopy sang their songs, along with the chirps and clicks of insects hiding in the undergrowth. It was these insects that were the geckos' quarry, each one a tasty delicacy that would be enjoyed at a weekly banquet this particular evening.

Sunlight created shafts of light through the rainforest canopy, making shifting patches of illumination on the forest floor. Thick vines draped like a veil throughout the area where Chase and Jonas hunted, and the humidity was thick and heavy as they moved silently forward.

Chase was now fully grown, along with his friend Jonas. Several molts of their skin had revealed their adult form, and despite Jonas' wound from their battle a year before, his scales had virtually erased the scar from the assassin that had tried without success to end his life. They had also matured, taking on more responsibility in the village, involved in everything that was important to the inhabitants of Andar and the rest of the realm.

The two friends were like brothers, never far apart in their daily lives in the village, spending every day together along with a female anole named Kiko, who made them a trio. The three were very close, and filled their days with both work around the village of Andar, and adventures of all sorts in the rainforest that they called home. Chase had enjoyed the peace and quiet that had come to pass in the year since the battle at Andoria. He did not like to think about the lives that had been lost for the Empire's greed and lust for power over the realm. But the Chameleon King had been saved, and the world had enjoyed a respite from the tyranny of Stigia in the meantime. The time of peace was good, and Chase and his friends enjoyed every moment of it, free of the thoughts of battle and death. Although he knew that things would not have been any other way, in the evenings when he reflected on those times, it filled him with sadness that it had had to come to an encompassing battle for the freedom of the realm.

His attention shifted away from the thoughts, back to his task at hand. He crept forward slowly and silently, with Jonas behind him, watching the undergrowth in front of him. He had spotted movement amongst the foliage of the jungle floor. The iridescent shell of a large beetle crawling across the mosses under the leaves of the greenery caught his vertically slit eyes, and he advanced silently, waiting for his opportunity. With a quick thrust, he speared the insect, hoisting the struggling beetle out of the undergrowth. It died quickly, and he stuffed the morsel into his pack, freeing the spear from it deftly.

"Nice one!" exclaimed Jonas, a huge grin on his scaled face.

"Yeah," replied Chase, "I think that should be plenty for the banquet. Let's head back."

Jonas continued to grin, watching his friend closely. Chase turned toward him, gathering the opening of his pack together and tying it off. He suddenly realized that Jonas was still grinning at him.

"What?" he asked, raising his arms in agitation.

"You don't fool me, pal. I *know* why you are in such a hurry to get back to the village. You miss your sweetie?" asked Jonas mockingly.

"Very funny. No, I just want to get the food back to the Great Hall quickly, before they spoil." Chase replied, holding up the pack full of beetles.

"Sure. Ok lover boy, let's go then…" said Jonas, spinning around and heading off without waiting for his friend to retort, a grin still firmly set on his scaled lips.

Chase simply rolled his eyes, knowing that Jonas enjoyed teasing him about all the amount of time he had spent recently with Kiko. The female anole seemed to hold an invisible grip on Chase, one which he could not break even if he wanted to. He just followed Jonas, not saying anything that might continue the torment from his friend about Kiko. They walked along the paths through the rainforest, making their way back home to Andar, the birdsong above announcing them as they went. Across a rough log bridge crossing a narrow spot in the river, it's cool, clear waters burbling past, and through the tunnel of vines and flowers which bordered the entrance to the village, and they were home. The village was busy with geckos and anoles moving to and from their homes and various buildings on the cobblestone which made up the streets of Andar. Before long, they arrived at the central building in the village, the Great Hall. All of the homes and business buildings in Andar were made up of round stone and mortar walls with thatched palm rooves, but the Great Hall was immense, a place for all of the reptiles in Andar to congregate for great feasts, and meetings. It was here that they met Lanwyn, the aging village elder. He was a Day Gecko, his bright green scales slightly paler these days due to his age. He rested in a large comfortable chair just outside the entrance to the hall, under a thatched wrap around porch which spanned from one end of the building to the other. He looked up at the two geckos from a scroll which he had been reading, smiling wide at the two friends.

"Looks like it was a good hunt!" he exclaimed, pushing his old body up from the chair.

"Yes," replied Chase, he and Jonas displaying their full packs, "It should be a very good banquet tonight!"

Lanwyn simply smiled, waving for them to follow as he entered the Great Hall. Inside, a fire burned in the massive stone fireplace at the far end of the room, and several torches cast their warm glow on the tables and chairs assembled for the banquet. It was tradition for the village inhabitants to gather once each week for a feast, to be together, share their experiences and discuss business important to Andar. Geckos and anoles would share a great meal, and the young reptiles and hatchlings would gather around Lanwyn in front of the hearth of the fireplace to hear grand stories.

Chase enjoyed hearing most of the stories himself. As he strode amongst the heavy wooden tables toward the back of the hall, with Jonas in tow, is eyes lingered upon everything, remembering when he was but a hatchling, listening to the elder tell tales of far off places and events that had happened long ago. Now, when he sat listening to Lanwyn tell his stories to the young reptiles gathered around the hearth, he knew that these stories were not so old… They were sometimes about *The Three*, the prophecy, and what he Jonas and Kiko had seen on their quests throughout the realm. To listen to the old Day Gecko speak about them was strange, like the three friends were puppets on some stage in the square in Andar. Although he usually chuckled as Lanwyn raised his arms during some climactic scene that he was describing to the young in front of him, his memories of some of those events were not pleasant. There had been times where Chase thought that they would not survive, and it had weighed heavily on him.

He brushed the thoughts aside, as they entered the kitchen at the back of the hall, unslinging his pack for the cooks who were ready to prepare the banquet. The geckos in the kitchen almost rubbed their scaled hands together, knowing that he and Jonas could bring back a better bounty than most of the hunters in the village.

Jonas did the same, and together they spilled the contents of their catch onto the tables in the kitchen, beetles and worms, small leafy greens for salad, and the occasional large ant. The eyes of the cooks lit up instantly, watching the buffet of insects flood their workspace.

Chase and Jonas had done their work, filling the plates of those reptiles who would attend the banquet this evening. Lanwyn smiled as he watched the kitchen staff get busily to work, beginning to prepare for the grand meal. Nothing was wasted. Whatever was not eaten tonight would be dried and stored. The rainforest provided much for Andar. Lanwyn finally turned and left, wanting his warm chair by the fireplace to sooth old aching bones.

It would be another night of feasting and stories in Andar's Great Hall, and as the sun faded above the jungle canopy, geckos and anoles alike started to find their places inside, as the fire crackled in the fireplace where Lanwyn sat comfortably in his chair in the heat from the hearth. The young ran about, and life filled the Hall with its sounds, as the night creatures began their songs in the humid undergrowth outside.

Lanwyn kept an eye on the goings on inside the Hall, smiling as he watched the young play, and the adults as the banquet was finally served. It was a good crowd this evening, and Lanwyn was brought a plate to munch away at as he let his thoughts drift to the story he would tell after the meal.

His eyes settled on *The Three*, sitting at the end of one of the large wooden tables. It had been another period of great peace, and the entire village was tranquil. Lanwyn watched them intently as he munched on dried insects. Chase and Jonas had been joined by Kiko, a female anole who completed the group. She and the two male geckos had grown up together, as indivisible as any friends could be.

2

In a remote village in the northern grasslands, to the west of the Sand Sea, a community of skinks went about their daily work. The buildings were all constructed of mud brick, fired in a large kiln sitting on the edge of the village by a stream which flowed through the middle of town. Each home and business had a roof woven of thatched grasses, and the streets were simple and rough. There were several small bridges which connected the village across the stream, a good spot to fish from for the local inhabitants.

The name of this small town was Sedda, and the inhabitants here mainly made pottery, which they traded with the mountain frogs of Nimisor, and occasionally Stigia, if they had a surplus that needed to be sold. The reptiles of the town maintained no real allegiance with any of the other races, preferring to keep to themselves in their quiet home on the plains. In the sleepy little village, life was fairly simple, although they did have a few soldiers, should the need ever arise to defend themselves. There were no outer walls around Sedda, it remained open to the grasslands which surrounded them for many miles. Even so, the skink soldiers were well trained, using the grasslands to conceal themselves from view, keeping a constant vigil over their lands while the citizens of Sedda went about the everyday work here. Young and old all took on a share of the work, and this community of reptiles was very tight-knit as a result.

There was no real leader, the reptiles easily governed themselves, and it was exactly the way they liked things. No one lizard made all the decisions, and even the males and females shared the responsibilities of raising their hatchlings and working around the village. In this way, no one reptile was any less important than the rest, from the soldiers down to the workers busily making mud bricks.

Life flowed along in a perfect balance in Sedda, and the skinks were always busy on a daily basis. The granary, with its large mud brick walls, and its thatched grass roof, was the central building in the village, always well stocked with food. The homes were simple, but arranged in perfectly straight lines along either side of the stream, the buildings aligned in blocks, with simple dirt streets. There was little decoration in Sedda, save for the odd potted plant on a front step, usually the same grasses that surrounded the village. The inhabitants saw such practices as a waste of valuable time, which would be better served by harvesting insects for food, or making more bricks, even fishing if there were nothing for them to do for a few minutes.

Time passed peacefully in the village, but the few soldiers would remain vigilant, always training to keep their swords and their skills sharp. The workers toiled away, either fishing or hunting, occasionally swapping jobs with the brick makers so that every citizen had knowledge of all of the professions needed in Sedda. The young were in constant tutelage of the skills they needed, and some of the stronger, larger hatchlings were chosen early to become soldiers. They combined their everyday tasks with training and swordplay. It was a well-rounded community of lizards, their town straddling the stream, and big skies stretching toward the horizon. At night, the stars filled that same sky by the millions, the planet's icy rings illuminated by the moon at times. Life in the grasslands provided the best celestial show in the realm, rivalled only by the skies seen in the Sand Sea.

It was home to this ancient race, the first skinks having discovered this place eons before, initially tunneling into the earth to find shelter. As Sedda began to become more established, the reptiles here learned to use the mud from the banks of the stream and manufacture bricks baked by the sun, with which they built the many building seen now. Their technologies improved, and with the kiln, its fire fed by dead grasses from the plains themselves, their bricks became even stronger, allowing for larger buildings like the granary. A few of the tunnels still remained, a reminder to each of the inhabitants where they had come from.

The Skinks of Sedda were a very proud and independent race, a group of reptiles who relied on no one but themselves. They had lived in the heart of the grasslands for many generations, preferring to keep their distance from the other inhabitants of the realm. Even the Empire of Stigia left them alone for the most part. It had been this way since time immemorial, and if the skinks had their way, it would remain that way forever…

~~~~~

Maxxus stepped silently along the paths through the rainforest outside the caverns of Andoria, The Chameleon King's friend and trusted advisor Ubius
~~~~~

close by as he strolled through the greenery. Maxxus had been distant today, preferring to keep to his own thoughts, something which had kept Ubius attentive to the King. His orbital eyes focused on each leaf and plant as he walked, his high casqued head never bobbing as they walked slowly through the undergrowth.

When something disturbed the leader of the chameleon kingdom of Andoria, Ubius did not miss it at all. He never pressed Maxxus, he knew that the ancient mystic would reveal what might be troubling him when he was good and ready. But there was something that occupied the Chameleon King's thoughts today, and it was quite obvious.

They walked on, and Ubius remained silent. He watched the King's distant stare. The myriad thoughts going on in his leader's mind was quite apparent.

"What is it, your Grace?" asked Ubius finally.

The King remained silent for long minutes, trying to find the words to express his concerns.

"I sense the continuation of the evil of Stigia. I don't believe that the new Emperor wants any kind of peace, and I suspect that we will see his hand at work again very soon…" said Maxxus.

Ubius took a few moments to digest what the King had said, walking alongside him through the rainforest. He always paid a great deal of attention to what Maxxus said, regardless of the time or place. He knew that anything that the King said was well thought out before it left his scaled lips. And the thoughts of Cyrus Malthor, as the new Emperor of the desert Empire of Stigia, wanting any kind of peace in the realm? It was crazy to think that there would be any rest from his tyranny or oppression of the other races for long. Ubius knew exactly where the King's thoughts were heading, and he had no reason to disagree with anything that Maxxus had said. In a few short days, the Chameleon King had convened a meeting amongst the leaders of the various races, in an attempt to reach a decision on what to do about Stigia. Maxxus was no longer content to sit back and wait for Cyrus to launch his attacks, or send out troops to enlist or enslave villages near or far. As soon as he had assumed the throne of Stigia, Cyrus had made his intentions clear to all of Evaria. Conquest. Once and for all. Where the previous Emperor had failed, he would find a way to rule the entire realm.

"We must convince the others that it is time to end the struggle with the horned ones," said Maxxus quietly as they continued to walk the paths through the rainforest. His colours flared momentarily, and he stopped, drawing himself up to his full height. The pigments of green and yellow of his skin becoming radiant and bright.

"Yes, Your Grace. We cannot wait for Stigia to raise another attack against us, or any other kingdom. Stigia must be stopped now, by force if need be. And it likely will be needed." replied Ubius.

"If Cyrus has his way, he will lay waste to everything we have all created, everything we have accomplished from the fruits of our work with nature. The new Emperor cares for nothing of this, he only thirsts for power and control." Maxxus continued.

The mystic could tell that this situation weighed heavily on the King's mind, that there was almost a sense of urgency to what he was saying. It was as if Maxxus could see the fate of their world, as it swirled in the passage of time. Ubius did not feel as though he had achieved anything close to that ability, but he knew for certain, that they must make the leaders of the other races share the vision that Maxxus spoke of.

The two chameleons emerged into a vine-shrouded clearing in the rainforest, immense and with a deep, bowl-shaped floor. In the center of the clearing sat a huge natural stone, a perfect table of smooth rock. It was very large, and around its edges sat seats made of smaller stones, one for the leader of each of the races of Evaria. It was a place of meeting, ancient and secluded, protected by the natural world.

"Send messengers to the other races, we should not delay in meeting." Maxxus said to his companion, as his eyes surveyed the stone table.

"Of course, Your Grace." replied Ubius, turning to leave.

The Chameleon King stood observing the clearing for long minutes, his thoughts consumed with what the new Emperor might be planning next, where he might send the armies of Stigia next. He was not certain, but one thing he knew was that the momentary peace they had been enjoying would not last for long. There was also another concern. Although *The Three* had returned the Gecko's Gate to Andoria after the battle of Nimisor, it still remained an object that the new Emperor desired very much. A powerful portal that would allow the armies of Stigia to travel across the realm in the blink of an eye was something that needed to be guarded, and hidden away from Cyrus Malthor and his Empire for all time...

~~~~~

Alibesh rose from her bed, knowing that this particular day was different
~~~~~

from the rest. In Sedda, each day was usually the same, with the normal flow of things to do for the inhabitants of the village. But on this day, the female gecko could sense something in the air, a change of some kind. It was as if something was reaching into her mind, pinching at her thoughts as she awoke to the sun shining on the plains outside her window.

She was an orphan, found almost dead after her family was attacked by a roving patrol from Stigia, the caravan of traders slaughtered by the horned lizards who were bent on eliminating the other races from the realm. She watched her mother and father, simple traders, struck down by the spears of the horned ones. The memory had stayed in her mind, as fresh as the new morning dew on the grasses of the plains. She had lived her life amongst the skinks of the village, had become one of them, exiled from the race she knew. They had taken her in, treated her as one of their own, and had trained her from her young age to fight.

This day she awoke to train once again, her sword at her bedside, ready and waiting. Its cold steel sang to her, and she slung it onto her back, a rough leather scabbard its home.

She knew that it would be a long day, already nursing the bruises of a previous lesson with the masters. But she also knew from their silent glances, that she was doing better all the time, was beginning to understand the art of combat. She had excelled in her lessons, surpassing her teacher's expectations with the sword. It had become a point of pride to her, despite the bruises she had endured.

Alibesh's complaints about the steel of her sword had fallen on deaf ears, her masters simply reminding her that she must become one with it. It frustrated her, as if the weapon would not become an extension of her will. It seemed to be the wrong sword.

She left the simple house of mud brick, grabbing a few dried beetles to snack on as she went. It was not a long distance to the training yard, where she knew that she would face a new lesson for the day. She stalked through the town streets, realizing that she was different than the other citizens who called Sedda home. It was impossible for her mind to escape the thoughts. She was an orphan, a gecko living amongst a race of skinks. Alibesh had been comfortable with it as a young reptile, accepting her adopted family's kindness. But as she grew through adolescence, it became more difficult for her to fit in. She had turned her concentration to her training, trying to turn her mind away from the thoughts of being an outcast. It remained in her brain, everyday lately. The others in the village paid no notice, accepting her rebellious nature without much question.

She neared the training yard, her thoughts set only on the lesson of the day, and who would be the unfortunate reptile who might meet her training sword today. She remembered the murder of her family. She remembered that she had been left as a hatchling to fend for herself. She remembered the brutality of Stigia and the horned legions.

Her thoughts raced even now, as she entered the mud brick gates of the training yard, ready to face whatever test her trainers had for her this day.

Alibesh had competed in many tournaments using a wooden sword, and her prowess for battle had become well known even in far-off villages. She had made her trainers proud, having never been defeated in the arena.

As the female gecko entered the gates of the training yard, her eyes were met a strange sight, and she stopped momentarily, her scaled hand suddenly itching for the hilt of the sword on her back.

Standing in the sand of the training yard, were two of her trainers, along with a taller reptile in a cloak. He was a monitor. She could quickly see that he was an assassin from the northern wastelands, and her mind registered that he was probably in the employ of Stigia. It made her uneasy instantly, and she shifted her weight, ready to attack if necessary. The monitor could read her moves, and his black, scaled arm reached beneath his cloak, most likely to a weapon at his belt. His stance stiffened, and his yellow eyes narrowed slightly.

One of the trainers could see what was developing, and raised his scaled arms toward Alibesh quickly to quell the look that he could see on her face. He knew that she had no love for Stigia, or the Empire.

"Ali… Stand down. That is no way to receive a guest." the skink said, quietly but firmly.

She relaxed a little, lowering her hand away from the hilt of the sword slung on her back. The monitor still watched her intently, but his arm returned from beneath his cloak, empty.

"This is Amilkar, who comes from Stigia to find you." said the trainer.

She remained silent, observing the monitor carefully as he nodded politely to her. Stigia. She had called it right. What did this lizard from the desert want with her? She looked him up and down, a slight air of contempt on her face. As if able to read her mind, the monitor finally spoke for himself.

"We have come to seek you out for your superior fighting skills. We have an important task for you, Alibesh…" Amilkar said.

"Why would I wish to be in the employ of the Empire?" she shot back, despite the look of warning from the trainer.

Amilkar simply smiled lightly for a few moments. He had been told that the female gecko did not often speak without being direct. But it was something that the monitor knew would help her in the job she was needed for. He could see the steely look in her eyes, her readiness to attack in an instant, if provoked. She would be perfect for what the Emperor needed, and he would have fulfilled his assignment. Amilkar grinned at her.

"Because you are exactly what we are looking for." replied the assassin.

3

Kiko waved down from the wooden walkway high in the trees at Chase and Jonas. The anoles had finally gone to work at rebuilding a treetop village in the canopy of the rainforest, not far from the gecko village of Andar. It was to be called Isimor, a nod to the leader of the anoles who joined their race with the chameleons and the geckos long ago to fight against Stigia in the Great Wars.

To Kiko, it was a vision from the past, a resurrection of the village she had never known as a hatchling. Her parents had fled the fires which destroyed it during an attack from the Emperor of Stigia's horned legions, and settled in Andar. Wooden walkways connecting homes and buildings built around the trucks of huge trees, high off the ground. A glassworks was central to the village, where beautiful bowls, cups, and various other containers were made.

"Hey! Are we going or what?" shouted Chase up at Kiko.

"Yes, already! Gimme a minute!" yelled Kiko.

Kiko descended from the trees on a spiral stairway built into the trunk of one of the ancient trees which towered over the forest floor. The craftsmanship that went into the construction of the village was exquisite, carved wood and woven vine ropes decorating the treetops. It had been years since the destruction of the village of the anoles, and none of the three could remember its name. All that they recalled was the stories from their parents of the fire burning the entire canopy, the entire village. It had been set by the armies of Stigia, by Cyrus Malthor and his troops. Many anoles died that day. For Kiko it had been more than just stories, she had lived the horror. Fire had consumed her home, taken her parents' lives, and as a young anole, she had been alone, in the care of the geckos of Andar. She was grateful for the village and being welcomed with open arms by the geckos, but there had always been something missing for her, a void in her thoughts. To her, the rebuilding of the village in the trees was a way of going back in time. She knew it would not bring her parents back, but it was a way of things feeling normal again. It put things on an even keel.

She ran down the staircase, jumping off of a portion that was still under construction, flinging herself out into open air some thirty feet above the undergrowth of the forest floor. Without apparent effort, she grabbed hold of a thick vine, twirling and sliding down it, and landed softly on the mosses in front of Chase and Jonas. She smiled wide at them.

"Ready?" she chimed.

"Yeah. It's about time. It will take us hours to reach the cavern for the meeting…" replied Chase.

They had been invited to the Chameleon Kingdom of Andoria for a meeting with the leaders of the races of Evaria. It seemed strange to them, they were not leaders of anything. But the Chameleon King had insisted on their presence. The Three would not be ignored in any time of urgency, with or without the prophecy that they had seemed to fulfill.

Kiko had a simple woven tunic on, a deep shade of purple today. It seemed to Chase that she looked better in the simple clothes that they wore around the villages on a daily basis than the silver armour that they had donned during the battles they had seen. Kiko seemed at peace in what she wore today, and to Chase, it was the look he liked best on her. She had also remembered her small packsack, which she always liked to take along if they went on a hike in the rainforest.

She grinned at them, sprinting off into the thick undergrowth.

"Waiting for you guys now!" she hollered behind her.

The two geckos exchanged a knowing glance as they headed off after her, both shaking their heads slightly. She eventually waited for Chase and Jonas to catch up, and the three friends began their journey toward Andoria, and the caverns where the Chameleon mystics lived.

It was a very pleasant day, the sun shone through small gaps in the forest canopy high above, and the companions were surrounded by the greenery of the jungle as they made their way through the foliage. Birdsong and the sound of insects filled the humid air.

Chase's thoughts turned to the Chameleon kingdom of Andoria, where they were headed. This meeting had been called rather quickly, a messenger arriving for the three friends in Andar just the day before. He wondered what could be so important, right at that moment, that required the attention of all of Evaria's leaders? It was probably not anything good, he thought. It never was. It also probably involved the Empire of Stigia, and Cyrus.

Just thinking about it made Chase uneasy, and he tried to dismiss the thoughts as he trailed along behind Kiko on the paths through the jungle. They came to the river after a short time, crossing it by a rope and vine bridge. The clear waters burbled past, and the friends could see small fish darting this way and that. Chase, Jonas and Kiko always followed the path, especially as they travelled further from Andar. Although the rainforest was beautiful, there were dangers hiding in the shadows of the undergrowth in certain places. The two male geckos had brought their spears just as a precaution.

"Are we there yet?" said Jonas jokingly, bringing up the rear.

"It isn't much further. We should be there within the hour." replied Chase.

"Good! I'm getting bored." said Jonas. "I wonder what's for dinner in Andoria tonight?!"

Chase rolled his eyes with a chuckle. Jonas was always hungry it seemed.

Kiko said nothing, happy to hike along through the forest quietly, looking around at the occasional colourful jungle flower. She too had thoughts about this meeting that Maxxus had called, and just like Chase, she knew it would not be anything joyous or merry. She hesitated to think what Cyrus could be up to now. One thing was clear; it was important.

The three friends eventually came to a mountain of moss-covered rock rising high from the forest floor and shrouded by the rainforest canopy. Beneath these rocks was the cavern of Andoria, the home of the Chameleon mystics. The companions loved to visit the chameleon realm, and sped up their pace, rounding the edge of the rocks toward the cavern's entrance. There was one guard standing on duty, dressed in shining silver armour, armed with a silver-tipped spear. There was also another chameleon standing at the entrance, dressed in the light coloured robes of the mystics. He turned to see the three lizards emerging from the thick growth of the rainforest. Their faces lit up as they recognized the chameleon instantly.

"Ubius!" exclaimed Kiko. "It's good to see you again!"

The chameleon bowed slightly toward her, greeting the friends the same way he always did, with a smile. He motioned them into the entrance of the cavern, with calm, kind words.

"The King will be pleased that you have arrived, he wishes to see you as soon as possible…"

~~~~~

The desert sun was hot and harsh as it reached midday, and Alibesh could feel her scales drying out. She hated the desert, and this journey to Stigia was the last thing she would have ordinarily undertaken. The female gecko walked
~~~~~

slowly across the sand, staying covered in her cloak as best she could, a very short shadow tracing her silhouette. The sun was at its hottest.

She was flanked by horned lizards, soldiers of the Stigian Empire. Amilkar walked several paces behind her, the monitor watching her carefully as they slowly traversed the Sand Sea. Her grassland home now laid many miles behind them to the west, the never-ending dunes the only thing in any direction.

Her trainers were amazed that Alibesh had agreed to go to Stigia so easily. They knew about her family's death at the hands of the soldiers of the Empire, and were surprised that the gecko had accepted whatever task that the new Emperor had in store for her, without hesitation.

But Alibesh had her own motives. She had said nothing, bowing to Amilkar in the training yard and graciously accepting his invitation. Her mind had raced with the sudden opportunity, and she had been very careful to seem grateful for what the assassin was offering. He had explained that she would be a great commander of The Emperor's armies and she would instruct them in the use of the sword, a skill she had obviously mastered. She had her own ideas, however, ideas that would have gotten her killed had she let them escape her mouth.

Even now, the plans swirled in her brain, and with the expanse of the desert to cross, she had a great deal of time to think about them.

As her scaled feet stepped through the sand, her mind was somewhere far off. She was a hatchling again, her mother and father beside her. They had been part of a caravan of traders, bringing spices from Andar to far off villages in the realm. They were suddenly attacked in the early morning, outside the marshes which crossed the borders of the grasslands and the rainforest on the western edge of the deserts. Horned lizards wearing the copper colours of Stigia ruthlessly killed all of the reptiles in the caravan, looting whatever was left. Alibesh had only survived by being absolutely useless. The soldiers were much more interested in real food, or precious metals and jewels mined from the mountains of Nimisor, and had left her to whatever fate would befall a lone hatchling out in the wilderness alone.

The skinks of Sedda had come across the young hatchling, crying and hungry, as she lay next to the bodies of her parents. They had rescued the young female gecko, bringing her back to their village to live as one of them. As she had grown, she could not bring herself to leave Sedda. It had become her home, and she had felt that she could never repay the kindness she had been shown by her adopted family. Although she knew that her kind lived in the rainforest in Andar, she felt a loyalty to the skinks of Sedda, and had been provided with everything she needed.

Alibesh had taken to the schooling of battle and warfare early, despite the fact that there was seldom an issue with the security of her village. Perhaps the training that she received, a form of ancient swordsmanship, was the very reason that no one approached the village with any idea of making trouble.

The female gecko had not been out in the rest of the realm much, except for the tournaments, but her stubborn determination to everything was something that her trainers simply yielded to. She was barely able to be controlled, even by those who had raised her. She had amazed those who had taught her, her moves were as quick as lightning, and her sword arm was like a serpent. She had never been defeated in the arena. But to Alibesh, the wooden sword was similar to a cane given to an elderly reptile. It was a handicap to her abilities, nothing more than some false show of her skill. She loved battle. Carving her way through a line of soldiers with bloody carnage was something that she longed for. Especially those reptiles that called themselves Stigian. She had only been involved in one very brief conflict, when her village was visited by troops from Stigia. But the skinks had simply made it clear to the soldiers that they were welcome to have a great meal, and move on. Alibesh had not shared their ideals, ready to make the steel of her sword sing, and the blood flow. Her adopted family had held her back, not wishing to have any issues with the Empire.

She had different thoughts, and this sudden visit by members of Stigia itself had presented her with an opportunity both timely and unique. Alibesh hated Stigia. And without being able to restrain her, the skinks had just allowed her to exact her revenge on those who had wronged her, without realizing it. The Stigian's were the ones who had actually brought the opportunity to her, like a gift.

The shifting sands distorted her vision, but she began to make out the spires of Stigia, unsure whether she was being fooled by a mirage in the heat of the desert. She raised a scaled hand to shade her eyes, trying to focus on the massive stone walls surrounding the city, the image obscured by the heat rising off the sands ahead of them in the distance.

"We approach the city, my lady…" said Amilkar.

Alibesh remained silent, trying to bring the desert city into focus as she walked. The walls of the city were the same colour as the sand of the desert, but she could see the dark stone which made up the tall spires of the keep, along with the monuments of the Emperor, and the groves of palmetto trees outside the city walls. It was amazing to her that anything could exist out here in this desolate place.

She was being brought closer to her vengeance, closer to finishing what she needed to accomplish. And they were foolishly doing it for her. She could sense her sword, set firmly in its scabbard on her back. It talked to her, whispering sweet sounds of steel and retribution.

Something stopped her thoughts as she watched the city come into focus, despite the waves of heat off the desert sands. Perhaps this was all a trap. The idea hit her brain like a hammer as she scanned the battlements of Stigia, and swept her gaze quickly over the reptiles escorting her.

"Go forward to announce our arrival. I am sure that the Emperor awaits us." She snarled at the horned reptiles beside her.

They went forward quickly, heading for the main gatehouse which would allow them entry into the city. Alibesh knew that should something bad happen; she could probably overcome the assassin who had come to seek her out. Once she entered the keep however, her chances of fighting her way out would become slimmer.

As they approached the city gates, Alibesh could feel her mind calling out for the hilt of her sword, and the automatic comfort it would bring in her hands. She resisted, keeping her eyes trained on the few soldiers manning the walls of the city, their vigil on her just as intent as hers on them. As they arrived at the gates, Amilkar stepped forward. The soldiers that had accompanied them stood in front of the gates, displaying their shields to the guards on the gatehouse walls.

"Open the gates, for the Lady of the plains!" he commanded in a loud voice.

The guards, seeing the assassin and the soldiers that were with them, began to move quickly to open the city gates.

The doors were ancient heavy wood, clasped by thick steel. They creaked open slowly, allowing the group into the city, and showing them a place of solace away from the heat of the desert. In the courtyard, there was a swell of activity, as troops gathered, following the orders of their captains. Reptiles moved everywhere, flowing like a sea. Never before had Alibesh seen this many soldiers, all outfitted in the copper armour of Stigia, swords and spears and shields in hand, ready to go into battle. It was an impressive sight, all shadowed by the massive statue of the Emperor, and the towering dark spires of the keep beyond.

Alibesh raised the hood of her cloak to observe everything. The guards, the gates, the walls… She needed to see the entire picture around her. Shielding her eyes against the strength of the sun, she cast a quick glance over her shoulder at Amilkar, to get an idea of where he was. They had just let her in, and they had no idea of what the consequences would be…

~~~~~

Maxxus waited very patiently, as the group of reptiles and amphibians milled about in the clearing of the rainforest, chatting with one another and greeting each other happily. It was a time of peace after all, and it had seemed like a millennium since they had shared time together. They had arrived over the last day or so, the leaders of the races of Evaria, from distant villages and cities. The area had been flooded with the leaders of the realm and their escorts and trusted advisors, all coming to the rainforest at The Chameleon King's request.

The new Regent of Nimisor had arrived just this day, Dukar's son Avik, along with an entourage of brightly coloured frogs from the mountain Citadel in the west. He was young, but reports had indicated to Maxxus that he was both skilled at leadership, and kind. He had rebuilt the mountain kingdom that had suffered immensely after the attack by Cyrus' forces from Stigia, and honoured his father's ideals of the importance of freedom in Nimisor. As Maxxus watched him across the clearing, he smiled, knowing that the power and strength of the mountains would be with him.

As Maxxus looked around the huge table of stone, he could see others that captured his attention. Taka was here as well, from the forests of Enderwood. The Salamanders had come once again, to show their support for the end of the tyranny of the Stigian Empire. He wore the wooden crown of his father before him, and Maxxus could sense that he would be a great leader of the kingdom of Kairn.

Lanwyn and Dalmus were present as well to represent Andar, along with one of the elder anoles to represent the new village under construction in the rainforest canopy. They chatted back and forth with one another, and it appeared that Lanwyn might be bringing this anole up to speed on the purpose of the meeting, and what might be discussed.

The toads from the Eastern coast were also represented, and Atrius of the city of Patima on the eastern coast sat comfortably at the table already.
~~~~~

The toad fishermen had brought a large shipment of fish from the Eastern Sea to Andoria, even though the chameleons had no need of anything outside the rainforest. It was a gift representing good wishes, and the mystics of Andoria had already set about cooking a great feast for the meeting of leaders thanks to all of the food that had been brought.

The Three were here as well, something which did not go unnoticed by the group as they milled about. Chase, Jonas, and Kiko remained quiet in a corner of the clearing near the Chameleon King, watching the procession of reptiles and amphibians from every corner of Evaria. They continued to bow and greet the various leaders, friends like Taka and Atrius, and all of the accompanying beings that came in their groups. It seemed endless, but the friends knew deep down that it was all necessary. Whatever Maxxus needed to discuss with the rest of the realm, they had definitely showed up to hear.

"Everyone." Maxxus' voice boomed in the clearing. "If we could please take our seats. It is high time to get to what we need to discuss…"

The others fell silent quickly, turning their attention to Maxxus as he motioned them to sit. Each of the leaders took their place at the table, ready to hear what they had travelled so far to discuss.

Evening was already falling, the rainforest becoming darker as twilight approached. Chameleons shuffled about the clearing, lighting torches around the large stone table of the meeting, and delivering light refreshments of nectar and dried insects.

Maxxus stepped forward, taking his place at the table, not the center, not the head of the table, but an equal. He sat down comfortably, Ubius emerging from the shadows of the clearing beside him.

"It is after great amounts of thought that I have called upon all of you, to come here and hear my thoughts. I also would like to hear yours…" he said slowly and carefully.

The others looked around at one another, not sure of where this conversation was going, or who exactly it pertained to. A sense of confusion arose, and there were murmurs between the gathered leaders. Maxxus could see the questions on their faces, and simply raised his hands for a moment to calm them so that he could speak again.

"We face an uneasy peace in the realm these days. I have been informed of massive troop conscriptions in Stigia, from all over the desert and the northern badlands. It is clear that the Emperor is building his war machine once again, and messengers have told me that they have never seen a larger army being assembled in Stigia since the Great Wars."

The reptiles and amphibians gathered around the table looked at Maxxus and each other in shock and dismay. They would never doubt the words of the Chameleon King, and this was not good news indeed. It was obvious to all assembled that their peace and tranquility would soon end, and the realm would be plunged into war once again. It was the work of Cyrus Malthor, the Stigian Warlord who has taken the throne of the desert Empire.

"We must send representatives to Stigia, to preserve peace and discuss terms with the Emperor!" exclaimed Atrius, the leader of the toads from the city of Patima.

"Cyrus Malthor will never negotiate on peace. He would simply kill any envoys we sent." said Avik, Regent of Nimisor.

The group broke into loud discussion back and forth, arguing about what to do, and what might happen.

"The Gecko's Gate must be protected, perhaps even destroyed!" said a toad.

"They might attack Nimisor again, looking for the sacred Eye of Nimisor!" shouted a frog.

"No, Cyrus and his armies will likely come straight for Andoria, to re-claim the Gate!" said King Taka of the salamanders.

Maxxus finally stood, raising his hands once again to calm the gathering. They eventually fell quiet again, shuffling nervously in their stone seats. He spoke in low, quiet tones.

"We could all simply defend each of our kingdoms, rallying our own forces to keep our defense individually. We could assemble one main army to face the soldiers of Stigia, wherever we guess that the Emperor might strike first. Or, we could use an object of great power to both lure and defeat Cyrus Malthor."

Around the table, looks of confusion surfaced again, and a babble of questions flooded the meeting, all in Maxxus' direction this time. He stopped them again with his hands, a look of patience on his scaled face.

"In order for you to understand, I must tell you a very old story, one that very few are aware or know of. I must tell you of a place in Evaria hidden away from the realm, where the remnants of the Great Wars hid a powerful weapon. One that might help us."

Maxxus sat once again, and began to tell all the assembled leaders about the glowing grove, with its pools of bronze liquid metal. He spoke of the time when Stigia had been defeated ages ago at the end of the Great Wars, when the realm needed to recover from its wounds. Battle had destroyed much of the beautiful world of Evaria, many villages and cities reduced to nothing more than smouldering ruin after all of the fighting. It was in the glowing grove where a powerful weapon had been hidden away for all time. It was a sword, forged in Stigia itself by the first Emperor and blessed by Shamans from the Eastern reaches of the desert. It was so strong and sharp, that it could slice through steel as though it were nothing more than cloth. The Sword of Xanth. Named in honour of the first Emperor of Stigia, it could help them in this time of looming darkness.

"But where is this glowing grove, and who will journey there to find the sword?" asked Atrius.

The others nodded in agreement with the question, looking to Maxxus again for an answer.

Maxxus turned in his seat, his gaze falling on three friends who stood at the edge of the clearing.

"I would think that it should be obvious…" he replied with a slight grin.

4

The Emperor stood at the window of the throne room, looking out upon the vast armies which filled the courtyard below. He stroked his scaled chin, watching as the soldiers fell into ranks, listening to the clatter of spears and shields. The late afternoon sun streamed through the window, warming his scales, the bright light reflecting off the sands causing him to squint. Shouted orders and the marching feet were the sounds that filled Cyrus' ears as he looked on, an evil smile creeping onto his face.

Word had already been sent to him that Amilkar and the young female gecko from the plains had arrived at the city gates. The Emperor was enthused, but cautious about the assassin's apparent find. A new commander for the armies of Stigia. He had heard of the gecko, a champion fighter in the arenas of the realm. She had never been defeated. But that didn't make her a leader, a commander. Cyrus was concerned that perhaps Amilkar had been blinded by her apparent beauty, losing his focus on his assignment. For the assassin's sake, he had better be right about this female gecko, thought the Emperor. After all, his very life depended on it.

The Emperor folded his arms behind him, his long black cape gathered around him as he looked out upon the city. Reptiles worked everywhere, moving busily from here to there, preparing. Preparing for their leader's plans for the realm. Preparing for battle.

Maps lay on the large table in the throne room behind him, spread to reveal the entire world that he had plans to rule. Colourful papers, drawn by the scholars and map makers of the Stigian Empire. Cyrus had poured over the maps and scrolls from the archives night and day, looking for any possible advantage that he could use in his campaign.

He had a great deal on his mind today, as he stood motionless in thought. He had struck an agreement with the leaders of the monitors from Nostria, in the badlands to the north. He was to be engaged to marry the daughter of this leader, strengthening the ties between the two allies, in exchange for large numbers of trained assassins to fold into the ranks of his forces. This turn of events had surprised many in Stigia, the populace hardly able to believe that the Emperor was capable of marriage, or of sharing power. But of course, Cyrus had no intention of sharing *anything*. This was not love, but instead a strategic arrangement. The monitors of Nostria were getting what they thought were stronger ties and a claim on the Empire with one of their own becoming Empress. Cyrus was getting an entire division of assassins to aid in his campaign, and had no real intention of giving the monitors anything at all, regardless of how beautiful his tall, slender bride-to-be was.

Regardless, it had created quite a stir within the walls of Stigia, and many servants were already busily working on the arrangements for the engagement, and a large feast, mostly supplied by the inhabitants of Nostria. There were meetings between the monitors and key members of the Emperor's personal staff every few days lately, to discuss what needed to be done for the engagement, and upcoming wedding.

Cyrus had finally waved his advisors away today, tired already of the discussions about it. He would have an Empress to Stigia in name only as far as he was concerned, and although he kept his own thoughts to himself, he would see them *all* dead before he would share his throne, or his power.

His thoughts were interrupted by the doors to the throne room opening, and a lone guard entering quietly. The other guards in the throne room remained silent and still, waiting for the Emperor to acknowledge the newcomer. Cyrus turned slowly, observing the guard without expression. Finally, he strode up to the platform above the polished onyx of the floors, and took a seat on his large black throne.

"Your Grace, the assassin has brought –" the guard began, bowing slightly.

"I know…" growled Cyrus, glaring down at the guard. "Amilkar returns with this female gecko, the fighter from the plains. Send them in…"

The guard bowed again without another word, quite happy to leave the presence of his Emperor. He turned quickly, exiting the throne room. Moments later the doors opened again, and Amilkar strode into the room alongside Alibesh. The assassin bowed deeply to his leader, but the female gecko simply stood fast, observing Cyrus. She had had her weapon taken before entering, but was still defiant. One of the guards stepped forward from his position at the base of one of the room's columns, swiping at the back of her legs with the butt of his spear.

"Bow before your Emperor!" he commanded.

Alibesh's knees fell to the polished floor, but she still did not bow. The guard raised the butt of his spear again, ready to deliver a second blow to the stubborn gecko. But Cyrus raised a scaled hand at him.

"Stop!" he bellowed.

The guard obediently retreated, assuming his post by the column as Cyrus rose from his throne, coming to stand at the edge of the platform. He glared down at Alibesh with smoldering red eyes, looking the female gecko over. She stared back at him, unafraid. He sneered at her.

"So you are the fighter that I have heard so much about, from the grassland village of Sedda." he snarled.

Alibesh remained silent, simply looking away from him without interest, instead inspecting the throne room around her.

"Answer him. It is not wise to upset the Emperor of Stigia." said Amilkar sternly.

"He is not *my* Emperor…" she replied sharply.

The guards let out an audible gasp at her defiant words. No reptile had ever entered this chamber and spoken this way in their leader's presence and lived to tell of it. But Cyrus just stood in front of her, grinning cruelly.

Amilkar lowered his head further, immediately regretting his decision to accompany her into the throne room, fearing that her insolence would earn him punishment as well.

"I thought this was the one that you had selected as the new commander of our armies, Amilkar." Cyrus hissed, turning his attention toward the assassin.

"The fault is not his, Warlord." Alibesh said loudly, her voice echoing in the vast room. "I played along with this game just to tell you myself that I would never do *anything* to assist Stigia for YOU. Your scouts were responsible for the death of my family, and so your death will come from me."

Again the sounds of shock could be heard, and even Amilkar gazed at her in amazement.

Cyrus stepped down from the platform in front of her, towering. He struck her quick and hard across the face with a large scaled fist, sending her sprawling across the polished onyx floor. She recovered quickly but stayed knelt on the floor. Cyrus pulled his sword from its sheath, hidden amongst the folds of his black cape, the steel singing as it emerged. He levelled the blade next to her throat.

"Your bad manners and foul temper do you no favours, gecko." said the

Emperor. "If I seem as just a warlord to you, you will learn a great deal over the short time you will remain alive. If all you wish to do is fight, you shall have it."

He slowly removed the blade, having already decided on a more appropriate punishment for her than immediate execution. She would have to suffer for her defiance. She would be an example to the rest of the realm. She would be a slave.

"Guards. Take the gecko to the dungeons to await her first fight. She will serve me in the arena of Stigia, whether she likes it or not." Cyrus commanded.

The guards surrounded Alibesh and Amilkar, their spears and swords pointed at them.

"What of the assassin, Your Grace?" asked one of the horned soldiers.

Cyrus looked at Amilkar with a sneer, leering at him for a long minute. His eyes flared with obvious disappointment in the monitor's failure.

"Lock him up as well. He has failed me once again, and will be executed soon enough."

~~~~~

Chase, Jonas and Kiko sat in the grove with Maxxus, their eyes wide with disbelief. Once again they had been singled out to take on something that they had no real wish to do. Would they now have to risk life and limb again? Chase slapped his hands against the smooth stone of the table in the grove in frustration. All of the others had gone into the cavern to receive the feast that the chameleons had organized. It was just Maxxus and the three friends out in the torch lit grove.

"You want us to go and find this sword, but you have no idea *where* the glowing grove is?" asked Chase. "And what about the massive army Cyrus has in Stigia?"

Maxxus sighed heavily. He knew that the three friends would not take this lightly, especially after all they had already been through. To throw them back into chaos, after this time of peace was a vile thought for him. They had accomplished so much, without any thought for themselves. They did not deserve to have to do *more* for the realm.

Maxxus cleared his throat, lowering his gaze from the three companions.

"I am sorry. I know of only part of the story." he said. "We go forward once again, beyond the prophecy of *the three*. Even despite my visions in the looking pool, I am lost this time. It is only assumption that makes me think that you three can find the sword."
~~~~~

Chase gave Maxxus a serious look.

"And why is it that you would think that we can solve every problem or impending battle that happens in the realm??" Chase exclaimed.

Maxxus simply watched the gecko, without answering immediately. He could feel the questions that the companions had. They knew he was uncertain of the future. It was very obvious that Cyrus was amassing troops for war, and once again, they did not know where he planned to strike first. It would be a separate discussion with the other leaders once Maxxus knew which of the other races were going to commit to battle.

"You three are free of the responsibilities of leading any of the races. You have no need for power or politics, and it makes you the best candidates as always. You always look solely to what is good and right." replied the Chameleon King.

Chase sat in thought, his scaled face knotted with concern. He had been enjoying the fact that there had been peace in Evaria. He glanced over at Kiko, who simply gave him a soft smile and shrugged her shoulders. He had enjoyed finally having time to spend with her. This new mission would change all of that now. He exhaled deeply. What would it take for there to be long lasting peace in the realm? But Chase already knew the answer to that question. No more Cyrus. No more Empire. But that was easier said than done. The races had been fighting the Stigian Empire since long before he was born, since the first Emperor Xanth had formed his legions from struggling horned lizard villages scattered all over the desert.

"I can only *ask* this of you three. You have done much more for the realm and the other races than anyone has ever done. I know it is not fair to ask more of you, but war is coming, whether we like it or not." said Maxxus somberly.

"So what do we do first?" asked Kiko.

"Yeah, where the heck do we even start on this one?" Jonas chimed in.

"There is one who may know the location of the Glowing Grove. You have met him before. The old toad who sent you on your way to Nimisor, who lives in the rainforest on his own." said Maxxus.

A flash of recognition crossed Chase's face. He remembered the old toad, he had given them new supplies of food, and sent them off toward Nimisor on the backs of Hummingbirds. He had known of their mission without them saying a word. Somehow, he had *known*.

"That's as good a place to start as any, I guess. The clearing where we found him is near the river to the north of here." said Kiko quietly.

"Great. Another crazy quest. We had better be taking lots of food!" exclaimed Jonas, stepping out of his seat and heading for the cavern entrance.

Chase, Kiko, and Maxxus smiled at one another despite the grim conversation. It was obvious where the gecko was headed. The smells of the banquet inside Andoria wafted through the forest, even out to the grove. Jonas' mission in life was food. If it wasn't for the fact that the companions were always on the move and active, Jonas would likely be very round by now.

Maxxus returned to being serious for the moment, knowing full well that Jonas need not be present to finish the conversation. The King knew that the male gecko would follow his two friends into oblivion if necessary.

"The longer that Cyrus Malthor remains on the throne as Emperor of Stigia, the more his hunger for power grows. He will not rest until he conquers the realm, and we are all under the darkness of his rule. We must act, and we must act now, if we are to finally stop him." said Maxxus.

Chase sighed. This was not how he had expected this day to go. Another quest had not been in his thoughts. Enjoying the company of Maxxus and the chameleon mystics in Andoria had been. Kiko put a scaled hand on his shoulder, as if knowing his thoughts. It was not what she thought would happen either. Their times of swimming in the river and quiet hikes in the rainforest were apparently over once again. They had entered into another time of needing to accomplish their task. The three of them would have to drop everything that they were doing, and take on this quest.

"I hate the Stigian Empire as much as anyone else. But I hope this is the last time we have to do something crazy like this." said Chase. "This should have been finished at Nimisor…"

Maxxus nodded in agreement.

"Yes, but no one could know that Cyrus would have survived his exile in the icefields, let alone had the strength to return to the desert so far to the north without freezing to death. And then to assume the throne of Stigia on top of everything else…" he said.

"His tyranny has to be put down for good this time!" exclaimed Chase, slamming a scaled fist into the stone tabletop.

"Yes," replied Maxxus slowly. "And you three are the ones to do it, once and for all."

5

It was damp and cool in the dungeon, and Alibesh sat on the floor against the back wall of the cell, keeping an eye on her guards through the rusted steel bars. Amilkar paced in the cell next to hers, restless and grumbling. Torches cracked and snapped in their holders on the sandstone walls, dimly illuminating the room. An old table and several well-worn chairs sat in the center of the space, and two guards lounged there, speaking together in low tones, chuckling occasionally as they glanced at the female gecko incarcerated in her cell. They were sipping from cups that had the reek of something fermented. The air was filled with the smell of the oils that the torches were dipped in to burn, and there was no breeze or draft to relieve it.

Time seemed to be suspended here, and Alibesh had only a vague sense of what time of day or evening it might be at the moment. Her stomach grumbled, and she realized that it must be later than she had thought. She had no expectation that they would be fed anything at any time soon, and what they might eventually be given she could imagine would not exactly be very tasty anyway. She tried to simply ignore the guards, and lose herself in thought for now.

But the only thoughts Alibesh could muster were from the day that her family was killed, by Stigian scouts. It had been a long ride with the caravan of traders, and they were already a long way from their rainforest home. She had been very young, too young to be involved in such a horrendous scene. The screams. The blood. She had been left amongst the debris and burning carts, a young hatchling crying over her parent's bloodied bodies. It was only after another day, as she looked up at the circling vultures overhead that a shadow had fallen over her. The strangers had taken her, fighting and screaming at first, away from the horrible place of death, and on through the grasslands to a village that Alibesh would come to know eventually as home… Sedda.

"Thank you very much for sentencing us both to death, lady gecko." hissed the assassin, breaking her train of thought.

She held no anger against the monitor, it was almost a welcome interruption from the remembrance of that day long ago.

"Perhaps you have resigned yourself to death, assassin, but I will not." she replied with quiet calm.

Amilkar grabbed the rusted bars of his cell, rattling them.

"You realize that they will put you in the arena tomorrow against an impossible opponent? Or perhaps several opponents? Oh yes, we will both die very soon!" he exclaimed hoarsely.

One of the guards thumped his fist on the wooden table, causing a clatter of the few pieces of cutlery and cups resting on its surface.

"Be silent, slaves!" he hollered in agitation.

Amilkar slumped down at the back of the cell, sulking. Alibesh did not change her expression, and the words that the monitor had spoken did not seem to affect her. She knew he was right, that there would be no fairness or sportsmanship in the arena for her. She had insulted the Emperor to his face, and refused to do what he was asking. He should normally have killed her at once for her insolence. The fact that he hadn't, and was delaying her end until he decided on something fitting for her acts of defiance meant that it would be very bad.

"If you had simply taken the job that the Emperor had envisioned for you, we would both have lived in great reward!" whispered Amilkar.

"You live a life of stabbing others in the back from the shadows, assassin. It is not your fault, you were raised and trained that way. I, on the other hand, have nothing to hide from, no need to deceive. I am here to cleanse Stigia, to force the redemption of its leader." said Alibesh.

The monitor leaned forward from his sitting position, resting his scaled forehead on the bars which held him in. The guards glanced at both of them again with stern looks, but eventually turned back to their conversation, and cups of nectar wine.

"Perhaps you don't fully understand. We will both die out there tomorrow…" he said solemnly.

Alibesh let her head rest against the back wall of her cell, looking upward absently at the sandstone ceiling. She could feel the blood pounding in her veins, she could feel the itch in her hands, desiring her sword.

"I can't wait for tomorrow." she said.

~~~~~

Chase, Jonas, and Kiko sat quietly at the grand table that had been set in the gardens inside the cavern of Andoria, munching on some of the food that
~~~~~

had been brought out. Chase was conscious of the glances they were receiving from some of the leaders seated at the table and could hear the suppressed chatter. Kiko glanced around, noticing the same thing. The companions were obviously a large part of the thoughts amongst the group. Only Jonas seemed oblivious, as he chomped away on dried beetles, swilling them down with a mug of nectar. He was in his glory.

It had already been a long day, and the three friends were happy to fill their bellies, and relax, surrounded by the quiet beauty of the cavern. Colourful wildflowers filled the gardens surrounding the table, and butterflies drifted along from plant to plant in the still, humid air. Chameleons came and went, clearing finished plates, and replenishing the food and nectar as needed.

Chase thought about what Maxxus had said as he munched away. It would not be so bad after all. They were going to try and locate a place in Evaria, hidden away for millennia, a place where no reptile had probably set foot for an age. It was another grand adventure for the three of them.

Chase looked up from his meal as a shadow fell across the dark wood of the huge table. Silhouetted by the sun streaming through the opening in the cavern ceiling, was the figure of a rather large chameleon standing in front of them, his massive arms folded in front of him.

"I thought you little geckos were never coming back!" boomed the chameleon.

The three friends recognized this muscled chameleon's voice instantly. It was their friend Dantis. Chase rose from his seat, reaching a scaled hand out toward him.

"It is good to see you again, my friend." said Chase.

The big reptile shook Chase's hand warmly, practically pulling him across the table in the process, his silver armour clanking as he reached across with his free arm to swat the gecko's shoulder as well.

"It has been quite boring here without you three!" he replied with a wide smile.

"Well, we certainly wouldn't want to see you bored, Dantis." said Kiko.

"Yeah. I see you haven't gotten any smaller!" said Jonas, still shoveling food into his scaled face.

"It has been hard to just sit here, guarding the cavern, without any action. The most interesting thing I have had to deal with in a long time was a bunch of slugs after the wet season…" said Dantis.

He sat down heavily, resting his considerable bulk on one of the chairs opposite the companions. Jonas slid a bowl of dried beetles his way with a warm smile. Dantis happily dug in.

"Things have been quiet for a while. I was hoping this time that peace might last a bit longer." said Chase, his vertically slit eyes wandering over his chameleon friend.

"Ha!" replied Dantis. "With Cyrus Malthor on the throne of Stigia, we will never see peace that lasts very long…"

Dantis slid the wooden bowl of food away, looking back up at the three friends with a grin.

"So I hear you three are going on another 'quest'. Do I get to come with you again? I want to get out and see some more of the realm." chuckled Dantis. "I am tired of watching the mystics practice their crafts. It's like watching the mosses grow."

Chase smiled, glancing between Jonas and Kiko. He remembered how the chameleon had enjoyed the adventures they had already been on. He had also saved their lives at least once. It was no surprise that Dantis wanted to go with them, Chase could imagine that in these times of peace that Andoria would not exactly be a place of great excitement or adventure.

"I am sure we could use your talents on our journey, my friend." Chase replied.

Dantis stood up from the table once again, just as Maxxus and Lanwyn appeared. Dantis immediately bowed deeply to the two reptiles.

"I see you have found your friends, Dantis." said Maxxus, his orbital eyes surveying the three companions, and his chameleon guard at the same time.

"Yes, Your Majesty!" replied Dantis. "We were just discussing the trip to find the Glowing Grove."

Maxxus raised a scaled eyebrow, turning toward the three. They had grins on their faces as well, at the chameleon's words.

"I was unaware that you knew about the quest I had detailed for *the three*. Perhaps I need to ensure that there are no other ears listening when I speak to them in private…"

Dantis said nothing in response, remaining at attention, even though his scaled face had clearly become a little flushed.

Kiko was clearly amused by his discomfort and chimed right in with the King.

"Yes, well, although he isn't all that smart, sometimes he comes in handy if there is a large log or rock blocking the path…" she said with a large dose of obvious sarcasm.

He shot her an irritated glance with one of his orbital eyes. She simply continued to smile at him, knowing he would not dare to say anything back while Maxxus was in his presence. But she also knew the look he was silently giving her meant that there would be payback later on.

Maxxus was still considering her words, also realizing that she was having fun at Dantis' expense. Despite being the King, he liked to have a bit of fun from time to time, as well.

"Why should I give up one of my strongest guardsmen for a task that the three are well able to handle by themselves?" he said, quickly exchanging a wink with Kiko.

The King could see the change in expression on Dantis' face, turning into a sad grimace slowly. Maxxus allowed the moment of torment to continue in silence for a minute, until the three friends broke into giggles at the big chameleon's look. Still, Dantis did not flinch, remaining stoically silent in the presence of his King.

"I suppose that Chase, Jonas, and Kiko could use the extra help and protection of a fine, strong chameleon guard, wouldn't you agree, Lanwyn?" he asked, stroking his chin mockingly as he turned to the elder from Andar.

"I suppose that might be a good idea, Your Highness." replied Lanwyn sheepishly.

Instantly, Dantis tried to conceal his smile and to remain at attention, despite his obvious effort to contain his excitement.

"Very well, we will leave you all to your preparations for your journey. There is still much to discuss with the other leaders. Dantis, you will ensure that the three are escorted to the armouries for their supplies?" said Maxxus.

Dantis was practically bursting with enthusiasm at this point.

"Of course, my King." Dantis replied quickly, bowing once again.

The Chameleon King and the gecko elder had barely departed as Dantis reached over the table toward Kiko. She deftly evaded his grasp, laughing. They left the table, and the few remaining diners who still sat at the large wooden table watched the jostling, happy group heading off down the garden paths. They made their way toward the stone building that was the armoury. Dantis almost skipped along, ecstatic that he would get to leave his boring post to perhaps have some fun at last. Chase smiled at him, but in his mind, he was glad that he would be with them. They had no idea what they might encounter on this trip, and having the big chameleon guard with them could be of great importance.

For a moment, he was taken back in time, watching the others as they walked along, the wildflowers lining either side of the path in the cavern. The laughter from his friends, the smells of the still air, and the echoing of sounds around them reminded him of a time not long ago when they had been here, and for a moment it seemed like he had seen this scene play out before him before. Maxxus referred to that feeling as a 'flashing-in-time'. It felt odd, and as he continued to walk, watching everything around him with sudden intent, the feeling quickly faded away.

"Are you coming?" Kiko called to him.

He had fallen behind, and with her voice breaking his train of thought, he took a few quick steps in an effort to catch up to them.

The friends arrived at the polished stone steps of the armoury, stepping up into the small building. The torches lit inside cast their light across the shining metal of armour and weapons, and on the far wall, The Gecko's Gate. The shimmering golden Octagon encrusted with gems hung on wooden pegs on the wall, underneath tapestries which depicted the battle of Nimisor, the creation of the Gate by ancient mystics, and the evil in the desert kingdom of Stigia. Some of the tapestries were recent, telling the story of the three, and it almost seemed surreal for the friends to look at them, seeing their adventures laid out in the delicate artwork. Their eyes fell on the Gate itself, it seemed too large for their eyes to completely take in. It glowed in its golden radiance, an ancient artifact which existed between the realities and far off places of the realm. It was like a central connection in time and space, and the friends could feel the magnetic attraction from it, could sense the disturbance it created in the flow of reality in the room around them.

Jonas sighed as he looked up to where their armour hung on several large wooden racks, made of beautiful silver. Their weapons hung nearby, as if waiting to be handled once again.

"The armour is so heavy and itchy!" he complained.

"Well, you had best wear it. It may help save you from another big hole in your scales!" replied Dantis sarcastically.

Jonas turned to him, knowing exactly what the big chameleon was referring to.

"Yeah, like it really helped last time!" Jonas exclaimed.

6

Alibesh let the sand fall from one scaled fist into another, like some kind of hour glass she had manufactured in her mind to quell the boredom in her cell. The hunger pangs had subsided for the moment, in what she could only assume were the early hours of morning. It kept her mind active for the time being. She had been unable to sleep, the damp and dusty dungeon not providing her idea of any kind of comfort. Amilkar was snoring fitfully in the cell next to her, and she did her best to ignore the sounds. It had seemed like an eternity in the sandstone cell, time marching past at a snail's pace. The amount of light in the room was exactly the same as when she and the monitor in the cell next door had been brought in, and as there had not been a change in their guards shifts, she had done the math in her mind to attempt to keep a basic idea of what time of day it was.

The guards were almost asleep at the dirty table in the middle of the room, and it was almost silent in the dungeon. The torchlight danced across the sandstone walls, in an abstract pattern that only added to Alibesh's confusion about the time of day it might be.

Sounds rose in the hallway that led into the room, at first faint. She could hear the clanking of armour, and a deep booming voice that she recognized quickly. The sounds became louder, and the slumbering guards awakened suddenly, trying to shake off their sleep and appear alert. The Emperor was coming, and from the sound of it, he was very unhappy.

Alibesh continued to pass the sand between her fists, as if nothing special was going on as the Emperor burst into the room with two more horned lizards accompanying him. Amilkar jolted awake, sputtering out dust as he struggled upright against the back wall of his cell, confused as to what was happening.

Cyrus stalked immediately toward Alibesh's cell, ignoring the assassin, coming to a stop outside the rusted steel bars. His smoldering red eyes glared down at her in the dim light of the flickering torches.

"You were brought here to be given a great honour, but instead you were insolent and insulting. All you had to do was accept the mission that was set out for you, and the rest of your life would have been like a luxurious dream!" hissed the Emperor.

Alibesh looked up at him, her scaled face devoid of any emotion.

"You mean *if* I survived your *mission*…" she shot back.

Cyrus' expression twisted in anger. He grabbed hold of the bars of her cell, rattling them as he spoke.

"You have begun to irritate me with your defiance, gecko. You will do as I command, or you will die in the arena facing my warriors. The choice is yours…"

Alibesh simply looked away, as if he was not even there. This enraged Cyrus even further.

"You will lead a regiment of my scouts into the rainforest and find the Glowing Grove. You will discover what is hidden there!!" He screamed at her. "Otherwise you will be skinned alive by my Stigian Champions!"

She turned slowly back to him, watching his every movement. His claws gripped the rusty bars of the cell tightly, and his every nerve was on fire. She could see that there was something that he was not telling her. Something that he was trying to hide. As she looked into his eyes, it slowly occurred to her, and a smirk erupted on her scaled lips.

"You don't know what you are looking for, do you? You only know part of the story? What is it that you want so badly from the Grove?" she purred, keeping her eyes locked on his.

He glared down at her, realizing that she was much more intelligent than he had given her credit for. He had given away information carelessly, and even though she was locked in her cell, it was not wise.

"When you emerge from this cell, it will be to meet your death. You will join your family." he sneered.

Alibesh did not change her expression, showing him no weakness despite the daggers that his words had become. She continued to stare into his eyes from the floor of the cell with no emotion, refusing to betray her feelings to him.

He did not wait for a response from her, spinning on his heel, and storming back out of the dungeon, ignoring the bows from the guards.

Amilkar scrambled to the bars, beating a fist against the rusted metal.

"Why would you not take his offer, and we would have been free of this place?! Even if you hated Stigia, and *me*, we could have come to some form of agreement outside of here!" he cried.

Alibesh ignored him completely, her gaze lost in space. She gathered more sand into her reptile fist, returning to her attempt to count time in silence.

<center>~~~~~</center>

The companions left the arched entrance of the cavern, heading off into the rainforest, their packs heavy with provisions for the adventure they were embarking on. It was very early in the morning, and there was a slight mist hanging in the undergrowth of the jungle, the sun had not fully risen yet. They moved off into the forest quickly along the paths leading away from Andoria, with Maxxus and Lanwyn watching in silence from the cavern entrance as the friends disappeared into the jungle greenery.

Chase knew that this adventure would not be an easy one. In the past, at least they knew where they were going. But now they had to go and find the old toad they had not seen for several years, if he was still alive, and hope that he could tell them more about this hidden place and its even *more hidden* treasure. If they could not locate the mysterious amphibian, or if he was already dead, then they would have no way to find the Glowing Grove. It would mean that the search would become much more complicated, if it would then even be possible at all.

He pressed on with the others, content for the moment to simply enjoy the sights and sounds of the rainforest while he expertly made his way through the jungle paths. Shafts of sunlight lit the humid forest, and large leaves stretched upward to gather its radiance. Despite their daunting task, Chase felt uplifted, enjoying the moisture-rich, oxygenated air and thinking about fun things to do while they travelled. He began to absently identify each sound he heard, whether a bird or the noise of an insect, almost automatic as each species was detected by his senses. He felt more at ease now, his strides through the undergrowth quickening as he became attuned to his surroundings. The others seemed to be doing the same, their pace much faster already as they moved in and out of the shafts of light piercing down from the canopy high above. Towering ferns, along with vines and the mosses of the forest floor, wildflowers growing out of the trunks of trees twenty feet in the air all greeted him as he sped along, minding his breathing and keeping his sword in its sheath tight to his side.

"Wait up!" yelled Jonas, unable to keep up with his friend's sudden burst of energy.

Chase kept going, letting out a bit of a laugh in answer.

"It's Ok Jonas, he will tire himself out, and we will have to carry him soon!" shouted Dantis, even further back.

Chase kept moving, dodging tree limbs and tangling vines, becoming one with the forest around him. He had always been good at making his way through the jungle with speed. But he didn't know where—

Chase was knocked aside, almost slamming face first into a tree as Kiko shoved him, emerging from the brush alongside him out of nowhere. He slowed, allowing her past him. She ran forward into the undergrowth again, her bow slung over her shoulder. He grinned to himself. She would never let him win.

He sprinted forward, trailing her through the leaves, feeling the soft mosses underfoot. She would not get far away, before he sped past her again, even tossing loose branches and detritus from the forest floor up behind him to slow her down. She let out a laugh, finally slowing her pace to let the others catch up. All Chase could do was run. He hoped he could outrun her. He hoped he could outrun the crazy responsibilities that had been put on him once again. He hoped he could outrun all of it. But he knew he couldn't.

He slowed his pace through the greenery whipping past him. His breath became easier as he paused, listening again to the rainforest. It was very quiet suddenly, and he knew that it was because of their running, disturbing the peace of the space they were moving through. It was OK. He let his body relax, felt his breathing slow as his friends caught up with him.

"So? Now that we are out here, what is the big plan, pal?" asked Jonas, stopping beside him.

Chase looked forward through the forest.

"Well, once we are at the river, we follow it, like before." he began. "And with a bit of luck, maybe we will find that toad again, and he might have the next piece of this great puzzle for us…"

Jonas put a scaled hand on Chase's shoulder, leaning in close to speak.

"Well, with a bit more luck, maybe you can concentrate on the quest instead of Kiko's backside, and we will indeed find something…!" replied Jonas, sprinting off suddenly before Chase could respond.

Chase clenched his teeth, almost laughing to himself over his friend's perfect timing with his wit. He silently planned a prank to play on Jonas at some future point in time as he again moved forward through the rainforest.

Many things poked at his mind, many questions about how they would accomplish the task which had been handed to them. He returned to his feelings of peace and serenity, even as he glanced back to ensure that Dantis was keeping up with them. He tried to push any thoughts of negativity aside, to remain positive. They would see their way to the end of this. They would succeed.

~63~

7

The Nostrian monitors were preparing to leave. The nomadic group was used to moving their camps, but this trip was different. A large caravan was being assembled, with a far off destination in mind. The desert Empire of Stigia. The northern wastes were alive with activity, even as the Lord of Nostria assembled his choice assassins to accompany the caravan across the Sand Sea. It would be a historic culmination of Nostria's dark arts, and Stigian military might. The ruler of the badlands was well aware of the agenda of the Empire of the desert, and despite those ideals, he sought to better his position in the realm by striking an arrangement with the new Emperor.

Amongst the politics of the mixed races of Evaria, this was a bold move by a leader. In a millennium, the Stigian Empire had been a strong entity, but the other races of the realm had been careful to either avoid dealings with the desert kingdom, or remain neutral to their thirst for conquest. Only the badlands had done any serious trading with Stigia.

The kingdom of the northern wastes had little to trade, their temporary villages surrounded by the scrub shrubbery and rocky outcroppings. The arid steppes of the badlands had served them well for generations, but many among the ruling class felt it was time to secure a more plentiful future for their race, free of scrounging the wasteland for scraps of food and water.

The Lord of Nostria felt that it was long overdue that the monitors cease ignoring the happenings of the rest of the realm, and take their rightful place among the more powerful of Evaria. The nomadic life the monitors had long enjoyed was no longer working well for them, and it had become quite evident. Food and water had become scarcer, and Stigia had held off recently on conscripting the finest of assassins from the guilds. The times had become almost desperate.

Yet the Lord of Nostria had set his mind upon a prize. One that might help the reptiles of his lands re-ignite their faith in the ways of old. He had struck the beginnings of a pact with the Emperor of the desert kingdom, in hopes that it would revitalize their homeland, would provide better trade and the flow of goods from Stigia, until the badlands could provide for them once more.

A great caravan was assembling, carrying everything that the Lord hoped would please the Emperor, offerings of food and supplies, an entire legion of assassins, and his greatest gift of all. His daughter. She would wed the Emperor, and unite the badlands of the north with the desert kingdom, ushering in a new era of wealth and prosperity for both races.

There had become few options for the Lord, and although he had always been neutral to the conflicts in the realm, it had become a time of sheer survival, and nothing else. He had held his head high, making the declaration of unity with Stigia, and assembling the caravan to carry out his commands.

And so, the caravan rolled out of Nostria, leaving the highland shrubbery, and the sandstone buttes of the steppe. The massive carriage built to transport the royals of Nostria rolled out onto the desert sands toward Stigia, followed by a dozen smaller carriages filled with food and supplies. A great legion of assassins, their training completed by the various guilds of Nostria, rode out with the rest. They had pledged their lives to their homeland, and to the Empire as well if they were accepted into its legions.

A large entourage of carriages, made for the long journey, and pulled along by giant beetles struck out on a great journey. Iguanas carried assassin riders out across the sands, along with the troops that Nostria had conscripted to stand with them on the voyage across the dunes. The Lord himself accompanied them, eager to strike a bargain with Stigia. Only a personal meeting with the Emperor would do in this situation.

The Emperor of Stigia had agreed to meet, and had accepted the idea of marrying the princess of the badlands, as well as increasing the number of paid assassin conscripts within his armies. Now had come the day when the monitors would venture to the desert kingdom to fulfill the agreement, and reap the benefits of closer ties to Stigia.

Perhaps the Lord of Nostria felt in his own mind that eventual change must come to their nomadic way of life in the northern wastes, that somehow the next generations of his reptile kin would be better served by making this pact with the lizards of the desert realm, and that somehow, his successors would return to the badlands and their way of life with a great deal more security and prosperity…

~~~~~

A beam of early morning sunlight shot down through the rainforest
~~~~~

canopy, catching Chase right in the eyes. He squinted, but kept moving through the jungle, following Jonas and Kiko, and Dantis. Kiko was leading them, because none of them knew exactly where to go, except to make their way to the river and follow along its banks as they had the first time they had met the toad. It had only been by chance that they had crossed paths with the old chronicler the first time. And did he even know anything about the grove and its secrets?

Chase tried to push the thoughts away as he made his way through the thick green of the undergrowth. It would definitely be a difficult task that lies ahead of them, and he knew it. If the old toad could give them some kind of way to locate the Glowing Grove, then they would at least stand a chance of completing this quest. Otherwise, they stood to roam the forest for a long time, perhaps never finding it to unravel its secrets.

Shafts of sunlight now lit up the jungle as they pressed forward, the humidity rising quickly. The friends could feel the moisture collecting on their scaly skin, and could feel the heaviness of the still air. Birdsong erupted from the canopy above as the morning sun rose higher on the forest, and the sound of insects surrounded them. Their pace slowed as the vines and thick growth became thicker, shadows mixing with the shafts of light penetrating the ceiling of the rainforest. Any remaining mist had cleared, but the weight of the moisture in the air was almost crushing. Dantis continually fought to keep his considerable bulk from being caught up in the thick growth, trying to duck down at times to follow in line with the others.

Chase subconsciously slowed his breathing, and slowed his physical exertion. This was definitely one of those days in the jungle, one where the heat and humidity could be deadly. A day where the trees and plants growing in the rainforest stretched upward, fighting for their piece of the sunlight above, bathing in the moisture of the forest floor.

"I can hear the river!" exclaimed Kiko, forging ahead through the growth.

"Good!! I need something to drink in this heat!" complained Jonas.

Chase grinned to himself, watching his friend fight his way through the greenery behind Kiko and Dantis, struggling to keep up. They were getting close to the riverbank, which was what Chase has been waiting for. It would guide them toward the spot where they had met the toad those years before, and hopefully give them an idea of where to go from there…

"Ok, let's get there and re-fill our canteens." replied Chase quietly, making his way through the brush.

He could hear the waters now as well, beginning softly as he walked, and growing steadily louder as the four lizards fought their way through the thick greenery. Eventually, the forest gave way to the mossy banks of a clear, cool river, narrow and shallow, its waters rushing past as the friends came to rest at its side. They sat down for a moment, to refill their canteens and have something to eat.

They were quiet for a long while, watching the water flow past them, catching a glimpse of an occasional fish. The sun shone down, illuminating the clear water right down to the shallow river bottom. Dantis breathed heavily, drinking his canteen dry twice, and eating voraciously, attracting subtle grins from the others.

Chase tried to remember the events that had brought them to the small clearing in the jungle where they had first met The Chronicler, the old toad who lived deep in the rainforest like a hermit. It had been several years, and the jungle changed rapidly, its mosses and undergrowth swallowing up the evidence of familiar places quickly. He searched the fog in his brain to see the places and markers which might lead them back to that clearing as he scanned the riverbank ahead of where they sat.

The humidity seemed even worse now, and Chase glanced upward to the canopy momentarily, his mind registering that it was nearly noon already. They would have to explore the riverbank well to find clues on where to head, before the light faded with the approach of evening. There was one marker that suddenly popped into his thoughts. A stone tablet, embedded in the floor of the forest, with ancient writing on it, warning them of 'The Guardians'. The traitor of a young chameleon who was supposed to be their guide had deciphered the writing on it for them just before abandoning them in a pit of quicksand to die. But it was years ago now, and Chase fought to remember everything which had led up to that moment. The Guardians, carnivorous plants which had tried to eat them alive, the fall into the river, being swept along… but how far?

Urgency gripped him, and he stood up, ready to continue on. The others could sense it, and quickly gathered their packs.

"We have to figure out where that stone is, you guys remember?" said Chase.

Kiko and Jonas nodded quickly, looking down the riverbank. Dantis simply waited to see what they would do next.

"And how far we went when we fell into the river after the fight with those crazy biting plants!" added Jonas.

Kiko nodded again, saying nothing but agreeing as the memories came flooding back.

"We had better start searching for that stone, before the light is gone." said Chase.

Without another word, the companions headed off down the riverbank, keeping a keen eye on the undergrowth around them, taking extra time as they went. It was painstaking and tiring, not like just walking through the rainforest. They lifted the leaves of draping plants, not wanting to miss a thing in their search. The young friends hoped that the 'Guardians' had not grown back after being cut down the first time. They followed the gurgling river as they had the first time, making their way slowly and methodically downstream, watching for any familiar sight alongside the cool, clear waters. It had been a couple of years since they had been in this area of the rainforest, and they relied on the river to keep from losing their way.

Chase sighed heavily as he watched the others move ahead, carefully scouring the undergrowth for any sign of the stone tablet. It would be slow going, he knew. At least this time they were not in a race against time as they had been on their last mission. Who even knew if this sword existed? Perhaps there was no Glowing Grove.

The gecko moved forward again, following his friends. His thoughts raced, and he tried to remain focused on the task at hand. One thing at a time after all, he mused to himself. At least there was no army of Stigian horned soldiers pursuing them. Yet...

All they had to worry about was finding the Grove... Before Cyrus... Again.

8

The desert sun was already high and hot as Alibesh was led out of the keep in chains, lowering her face and squinting to shield her eyes from the sudden bright light, as well as the stares of the reptile citizens of Stigia. There was no throwing of fruit or vegetables at her, no screams of her being a defilement to what the Empire stood for. The female gecko was not surprised by this. Here in Stigia, the citizens would not part with any food, even if it was half rotten, lest they might starve the following day. And although they were obedient to rule, they did not shout out in support of it. She had ignored the Emperor's requests for two days, infuriating him to the point that he had decided to keep to his word about forcing her to fight. The Stigian arena was on the east end of the walled city, next to the barracks and the armouries. Amilkar was practically being dragged along behind Alibesh, also shackled. She paid no attention to him or the guards who led them onward, instead taking in every detail of the city as she walked. Horned lizards scurried in every direction, anxious to keep out of the soldier's way as they performed their tasks.

Alibesh knew what was ahead. There would be no wooden swords in this arena. Stigia's reputation for brutal exhibitions with real weapons and real blood was legendary, a tradition supported by each emperor who had assumed the throne of the Empire. To be victorious in battle in the arena meant that a soldier would be considered among the elite of Stigia's armies, and many had died trying to achieve such recognition. Only the most highly skilled and experienced fighters would dare enter, as the arena was ruthless as much as it was bloody.

Her thoughts were interrupted as one of the guards yanked on the rope tied to her shackled wrists, dragging her suddenly forward. She did not change her expression to give the guard the satisfaction that he had affected her in any way.

They continued through the city streets, and the two captives remained the center of attention to passing citizens. Alibesh watched without attracting attention as they passed the stables. Inside she could see large Iguanas and tortoises ready to be saddled. But her eyes came to rest briefly on wasps, ready to take wing once untethered and brought out into the open air. She had but a moment to see them, the guard yanking on her restraints again. She lowered her gaze so as not to allow her captors to realize what she was looking at.

As the entourage drew closer to the arena, Alibesh could hear the shouts and cheers, punctuated by the clash of steel. As they met with the back of the crowd gathered around the battle, Alibesh could feel eyes upon her. She turned, looking back behind her, seeing only Amilkar and the remainder of the guards escorting them, the citizens in the streets nothing more than an unfocused blur. Her eyes went upward, to the dark spires of the keep. There stood a dark figure high above, staring down at them. It was the Emperor. Alibesh stopped in her tracks for a moment, returning his stare defiantly, until the guards yanked her by her bonds, pulling her forward once again.

The crowd parted for them, still jostling and shouting at the fighting already engaged in front of them. The lizards near them stared at Alibesh in disbelief as she was led through them toward the outer stonework of the arena. They halted at the edge, looking down into a pit with a sand bottom, surrounded by elaborate stone walls separated every ten feet by columns. The crowd peered down at two reptile combatants, fully armoured and armed with swords. One of them was a horned lizard, clad in the copper metal of the soldiers of the Stigian army. He had a copper shield along with a short sword, dodging the swings of his opponent. His adversary was taller and slender, a monitor from the badlands to the north. His armour was a dull, unpolished steel, and the long sword he clasped was curved cruelly. They danced around and toward one another in successive clashes, the crowd cheering them onward.

Alibesh watched with interest, even as she felt the stares of some of the spectators upon her. Her vertically slit irises observed the two reptiles fight, her brain registering each move, each strike and defense in a very analytical way. It was second nature to her. And she was very aware of who would be tasked with fighting against the victor in the battle before her. SHE would be the next to enter the arena. She could still sense the Emperor watching her, waiting to see if she would give in and submit to his wishes. She dismissed his gaze, pushing the thought from her mind. Alibesh knew that it would only aggravate him further to be ignored. It brought the slightest beginnings of a grin to her scaled face as she watched the fight continue. Her hands ached restlessly for her sword. She could feel her pulse quicken slightly, could hear her own heartbeat in her ears as she watched the two fighters attack each other again and again. Sand flew as they lunged back and forth in the arena, each strike and parry of steel bringing a noisy reaction from the crowd surrounding them.

The heat beat down mercilessly. The clash of metal, the grunts of effort played out in slow motion in front of her. It was a ballet in her mind, and her eyes watched each move, each muscle of the two fighters. Her analysis suddenly shifted gears, and she began to see the openings that they left in their defense. Momentary holes that Alibesh knew she would have capitalized on in combat. Instantly.

Her grin grew a bit wider as she continued to watch the exhibition. What more could it be? They were amateurs at best. The horned lizard of Stigia lunged forward in short-sighted attacks, while the monitor defended, trying to use his height as an advantage over his shorter rival.

"This is where we will die." whispered Amilkar from behind her.

She barely turned her head, eyes still on the arena as she listened.

"You should have taken the Emperor up on his offer, in the future, you might have been his most trusted commander, and I would be free to return to my homeland." he continued.

"You just make yourself ready and do exactly as I say if you wish to live…" she replied quietly.

One of the guards shoved them violently, with a command to be silent. Amilkar nearly fell to the ground, and Alibesh fired back an angry look at her captor. She would ensure that the guard was the *last* to die. No one laid a claw on her without paying a price.

Her attention was forced back to the arena as a sudden scream penetrated the crowd, the onlookers cheering loudly as the monitor drove his curved blade between the copper plates of armour of the horned soldier, having capitalized on a momentary opening in his adversary's defenses. Blood spurted from the large wound as the lizard fell to a knee, wrapping a clawed fist around the steel still protruding from his scales. Finally, the monitor yanked his sword free of his enemy's flesh, and blood sprayed across him and the sand of the arena floor. The cheers were thunderous. The victor raised his arms, bloodstained, with his sword held high in display to the gathered crowd. They continued to shout and chant, coins quietly changing hands.

The monitor turned slowly toward the guards at the side of the low arena wall, and to the female gecko. He glared at her coldly, wiping blood from his curved blade, his eyes remaining trained on her. A grin erupted on his scaled lips, as he motioned to the guards, ready to fight again.

Alibesh was shoved again, forward this time toward the edge of the arena. One of the guards drew his sword, leveling it at her throat, another removing her shackles. A small gate in the low stone wall was opened, and she was pushed through, tripping and landing on her knees in the sand. She stood up, casually brushing the sand from her knees and legs as she locked eyes with the monitor across the arena from her. She had no weapon, no armour. The crowd began to taunt and jeer at her. She could hear some of their words; *"What was a female doing here?"* and *"Filthy gecko"*. She ignored them. She turned toward the guards, keeping one eye on the monitor as well.

The guard who had held the sword to her throat moments ago, smiled cruelly at her. He tossed that same sword into the arena now, where it landed in the sand a few feet from her. The crowd laughed, watching the female gecko stoop to retrieve the weapon from the sand. She straightened, turning back toward her enemy, squaring off in front of him in a classic defensive position, the sword at the ready.

The crowd quieted themselves, and the monitor raised a scaly eyebrow at her as his grin diminished slightly. He shrugged off his caution, raising his sword threateningly, preparing to charge straight at her. Time seemed to slow, and the female exhaled deeply. The moment had come. That moment when the battle would be joined, and each move and countermove was important. Alibesh closed her eyes, listening to every sound around her, and gestured the monitor forward, mockingly. This enraged her adversary, and he let out a bellow as he strode quickly across the arena floor toward her, outstretching his sword arm in full attack, his head lowered as he came at her.

Her pulse had slowed, and she kept her eyes shut, listening for each footfall across the sand that the monitor made above the cry of his voice charging toward her. Her muscles relaxed, and she remained unmoving, feeling the heat of the desert sun from above, hearing the cheers of the crowd demanding her death.

It would end just as quickly as it had begun, in a space of seconds which seemed to stretch into eternity in her mind. In a masterpiece of speed and dexterity, she made a quick sideways step, opening her eyes as she swung the sword hard in an arc perpendicular to his line of attack. She watched as his sword went past her face, missing its mark as her blade severed down into the flesh of his scaled neck. Blood sprayed everywhere, and the monitor's body fell forward and past her, his head rolling into the sand by her feet. His clattering armour was the only sound for a moment, as the crowd went silent in disbelief. She had killed him with only a single swing of her sword. The silence came to an end as the crowd erupted in booing and shouting, angered at the unexpected defeat of their chosen champion.

Alibesh did not wait for them to be able to react further, as she had spotted the guards' sudden confusion. She leapt forward, landing on the stone wall of the arena, and jumped straight forward over top of the guards, doing a somersault in the air above them. She landed behind them, and as they swung around to try to see where she was, she sliced her sword down through the restraints that held Amilkar, two steps away. The guards moved forward, attempting to draw their weapons. All except the one guard who had no weapon. He had given it up to her and was now far too close to her.

She slit his throat with his own sword, blood showering them and several reptiles among the crowd. Lizards stumbled to back away over one another, panicked by the sudden attack. As the guard's body fell, Amilkar wasted no time. He sprinted away from the arena, with Alibesh following directly behind. The remaining guards plowed forward, fighting through the reptiles, until they were able to pursue down the cobblestone street.

There was no place to hide, as they streaked down the street. Sandstone buildings and scared citizens flashed past them. The gecko was not worried about hiding. They had to get out of the city and get out now. She could hear screamed commands from somewhere in the keep high above, and without looking, knew that it was the Emperor in the large window of the throne room, shouting in anger to his soldiers who were following them. They did not have much time. Their chances of escape would grow smaller with each passing minute, as the sound of horns arose, signaling other guards around the city walls.

Alibesh saw her target, at last, catching up with Amilkar, yanking him to the side of the street and into a nearby building.

"What are you doing?? We have to keep moving!" he exclaimed, looking at her in disbelief.

"We will be dead long before we ever make it near the city gates. We need to get off the street." she replied calmly.

They stepped through the large open doors of the building, wary of what might be inside. Now Amilkar could see what Alibesh had planned. They were in the stables, and several large wasps were tied up, already saddled for flight. He didn't even have the chance to say anything, and felt the heavy blow of the female gecko's sword against the back of his head. He fell to the cobblestone floor, and felt himself being dragged into a pile a straw in the corner of the room.

"When night comes, you can use your talents, and the shadows to escape, Assassin…" he heard as his consciousness faded.

Alibesh mounted the nearest wasp, cutting loose the reins with her sword. Its large wings flicked with a droning sound, and it leapt into the air, and out of the stables.

Arrows sliced the air around her, and Alibesh tossed the sword out into open air, preferring to hold the reins of the insect she rode, tightly. They rose quickly out above the walls of the city and into the hot, dry desert air, Stigia fading behind them quickly. She dared not slow her mount, however, as she could hear another sound above the drone of the wasp's wings. She glanced back just for a moment, and realized quickly by seeing three more dots above the Sand Sea, that she was being followed…

<div align="center">~~~~~</div>

The 'Chronicler' as he was known observed the three friends suspiciously, his dark bulbous eyes fixed on them as he toyed with his pipe. A small fire lit the clearing as darkness began to fall, illuminating the amphibian as he reclined by a clump of large mushrooms. A cloud of aromatic smoke surrounded him, along with a better part of the clearing. His gaze told Chase that he had been expecting company today, perhaps even the very reptiles who now stood in front of him…

He did not resemble his kin from the shores of the Eastern Sea in Patima, being much larger and fatter. His eyes were also larger, and even the patterns on his warty skin were different. Perhaps he had evolved differently here in his jungle home. If that were true, it would mean that he was very old indeed, and had lived here for a long time…

Chase waited patiently, hoping the old toad would remember them. It had been several years after all, and the three of them had grown since they had last seen him. He had to remember them. Their accomplishments must have reached him, especially if he was 'The Chronicler'.

Smoke swirled around the old toad as he reclined beneath a large mushroom, savouring his pipe. Splotches of colour covered his warty skin, his throat billowing in and out with each breath. When he blinked, which was seldom, his eyes would almost sink downward into his head, resurfacing quickly. Stubby arms ended in thick fingers, one hand grasping his pipe, the other resting against the fat of his sides.

"What is it you seek me out for?" asked the toad in a gravelly voice.

The three friends looked at one another for a moment, half expecting that the aged amphibian knew the answer already.

"We need to know how to find the Glowing Grove." replied Chase calmly.

The toad's eyes seemed to widen slightly, and he coughed suddenly on the smoke from his pipe. He looked at each of them intently, and an awkward silence passed before he spoke again. He grunted slightly, finally replacing the pipe in his wide mouth.

"And why do you wish to venture to the forest of light?" he asked.

"There is something hidden there that we need..." said Kiko, stepping forward slightly.

The toad's eyes again grew wide.

"You may need it, but none of you are able to remove it from its hiding place!" he scowled at her. He watched their reaction to his words carefully, his eyes surveying their body language, their expressions. He raised one of his eyes slightly higher as he watched them.

"And none of you know what it is you are looking for!" he boomed suddenly.

The three companions stared at him silently, knowing looks appearing on their scaled faces, despite their attempt to hide them.

Chase took the situation in hand, doing his best to sound both respectful and firm.

"We have been sent on this quest by Maxxus, the Chameleon King of Andoria, and we-"

The old toad rose from his reclined position in a flash, stepping toward the gecko without hesitation, tossing his pipe aside.

"I know who you are young gecko... and who has sent you!" he shouted.

His bulbous eyes surveyed the three once again, and he stepped back again toward his mushroom.

"I know well the story of the three, and you must know now that you live beyond the prophecy, beyond a time where only a few might be able to see your fate." the toad said, his voice becoming calm again.

Chase could not understand why the toad was so agitated. The last time they had met him, he had seemed nothing but helpful and kind. It was as if the three friend's existence messed up what the toad saw as the way the world around them should be. The gecko knew that the prophecy was over with, that they had survived to see it fulfilled, and that from that point on they had been in uncharted territory.

The chronicler paced slowly around the clearing, obviously in deep thought. He had retrieved his pipe, and puffed away on it as he waddled back and forth, muttering to himself incoherently.

Kiko had an irritated expression now, as well. Chase could see it develop, and despite his attempts to get her attention, she had ignored him. She glared at the toad as he stalked slowly around the clearing. They were not some idiot lizards who should be treated like hatchlings, she thought angrily. They had risked their lives even trying to find this amphibian, after all. It was not like they were out for some type of personal gain, they were trying to once again help the entire realm it seemed!

"Look! We came to find you to get your help! If that isn't what you want to do, perhaps we should leave you to yourself here in the middle of the jungle!!" shouted Kiko angrily.

The toad stopped dead in his tracks, looking up at her in wonder. His expression quickly softened into a subtle grin.

"I am sorry if I offend you, young one." he began. "Of course my intention is to be of service to you. The problem is not the location of the grove."

He turned, waddling back toward the large clump of mushrooms at the end of the clearing. Reaching into one of them which seemed to be hollowed out, he withdrew a large leaf-bound book. It was beautiful in its natural design, the cover made of huge dark green leaves, which had somehow been preserved perfectly. The Chronicler opened it, flipping rapidly through its crinkling pages, obviously knowing exactly where he needed to read from the thick tome.

Chase exhaled finally, realizing that Kiko's words had not enflamed the situation, but had somehow set things back on an even keel. Dantis and Jonas seemed more relaxed now as well.

The toad pulled out a large pair of strange looking glasses from between the pages of the book, placing them on his warty face with a slight grunt of approval as he scanned the open pages. After a few moments of grumbling slightly as he read the words to himself, he spoke again.

"It is the one who bears the mark of the diamond who will be safe from the liquid fire, the one who will return with the sword, to be obedient to its work, to its course in the cosmos. Without fear, the warrior will change the course of the realm, the course of Evaria for all time..."

As the toad finished reading, a silence fell on the forest surrounding them. Even the birds seemed quiet in the canopy high above. The four friends digested what the toad had said. None of them could retrieve this sword, none of them could complete this quest.

The toad looked up from his book, removing his glasses and giving them a very sober gaze.

"This is what I was trying to tell you, and I have said this to Maxxus, as well. None of you bear the mark." he said calmly.

Chase's spirits began to sink. He glanced at the others, who seemed to share his disdain. He lowered his gaze to the ground, lost in thought. Why would Maxxus send them on a mission that he knew they could not finish, one that was impossible? Surely there was an explanation to this craziness, one that would make sense.

As if sensing their confusion, the old toad continued to speak, slapping the large book closed as he began again.

"Perhaps the Chameleon King sees something during his meditations that escapes me, as he is insistent that there is a way to retrieve this artifact. I, for one, am not sure that it should be found at all..."

He looked around at all of them once more.

"Some things should be left to the ages, and not be disturbed..." he said.

The friends remain silent for a considerable time. Many thoughts crashed over them like waves, as the realization hit them that this would be much more difficult than they had ever imagined. Maybe Maxxus had known this all along and kept it from them, maybe there was a part of this particular quest in which he had doubted their resolve. Whatever the case may be, they knew that it was far too late to quit and go home now.

"Is there anything else you can tell us about who might have this mark?" asked Chase.

The toad focused his large bulbous eyes on the gecko. A sudden sadness flashed across his ancient wart covered face, as if he was somehow reading the future that was in store for Chase and his friends at that exact moment in time. Chase could suddenly feel a chill in his scales, as if he were asking more than he should of The Chronicler. Had he stepped out of where he should be with his question? He could see his friends fidget slightly out of the corner of his vision, and he knew that they could feel the sudden awkward moment in the conversation. The toad continued to look at Chase intently, as if reading his thoughts. After a moment more, he simply turned away from them, stepping back toward his clump of mushrooms. He replaced the book where it had come from, and retrieved his pipe, re-lighting it with a stick from the fire. Several puffs later, the smoke filled the clearing once again, and the friends tried again not to appear rude by stifling the urge to cough. He still faced away from them, and it was clear that he was thinking, his mind somewhere else. Finally, he turned back to them, as if he had made peace with what he might be about to say. Another puff on the pipe, and he spoke at last.

"Rest now, for tomorrow is already coming. I will give you all that you need, both in knowledge and supplies. I hope that Maxxus is right about this, but whatever is destined to happen, I am sure that I will need to begin a new chapter in the histories of this world..."

9

Amilkar shook his head slightly, trying to clear the fog from his mind in the darkness of the pile of straw he was concealed in. It was quiet, except for the occasional hum of wings as the wasps exercised them for short moments.

The monitor knew that he must get away from the city, and that if he was found by the Stigian soldiers, he would most certainly not survive another day. He had been lucky that the Emperor had allowed him to live after his first failure. This time, there would be no reprieve for him.

He sat up slowly, peering around the stables cautiously as the straw fell away from him. It was dark in the room, except for the light from a single lantern near the doors at the far end of the narrow stone building. There were many makeshift stalls, each containing a resting wasp, fully outfitted with saddle and reins. It was equally dark outside the windows of the building. Night time. He breathed a slight sigh of relief. It would be much easier to move about under the cover of darkness. He was grateful to be in one piece, a fact which he credited to having been rendered unconscious by the treacherous female gecko. She was the reason he had been reduced to this. A flash of anger crossed his mind as he considered everything that had happened since they had arrived here in Stigia. But the assassin brushed it away, knowing that he must concentrate on escape from this city before he concerned himself with anything else. It was time to survive first.

He stood shakily, rubbing the bruised, black scales on his head. Cursing under his breath at Alibesh, he moved silently toward one of the windows. The hour must have been late, he assumed, because the cobblestone streets were absolutely deserted. This would help him as well, and luckily, his training in the guilds of Nostria had centered around an ancient assassin art called *The Unseen*. He would be able to keep himself invisible long enough to escape.

Amilkar looked around, considering the idea of simply leaving quickly on the back of one of the wasps as the female gecko had obviously done. The stall nearest the main doors was empty, as were the next three. They had pursued her… he registered in his brain. He did not want the same for himself. No one knew he was here still, and if he didn't raise the alarm with a late night fly-out over the walls, where there would most certainly be guards, he could slip away unnoticed into the night without any of the soldiers in pursuit.

He needed two things: he needed a lightweight cloak, to protect him against the sun when morning came, and he needed water for the trip across the Sand Sea. One of the wall guards might have both of these. A weapon of some kind might also help but was not really necessary.

Amilkar moved down toward the doors without a sound, his head having cleared now. He opened the door very slowly, peeking out to ensure no one was lurking outside. His slid out the doors and around to the side of the building, where the shadows were darkest and away from torchlight. He was now relatively safe for the moment, no longer trapped in the stables, and completely invisible. He surveyed the street in front of him, watching for long minutes. Nothing moved and the arid desert air was still. There were no soldiers, but he knew that he had to assume that there were patrols throughout the city, which he might have to avoid.

He spotted something down the street that would suit his needs. It was a stone-walled well. He slid himself along a high stone wall in the darkest shadows, working his way past silent vendor's stands and wagons. His sharp vision assisted in helping him remain silent and stealthy as he crept down the street toward the well. It was out of the shadows, so he would have to be careful. A torch on a wall opposite him shed more light on the well than he would have liked, and he had no way of extinguishing it from where he was.

He hesitated a few moments, listening and watching the darkened streets. Shadows crept along the cobblestone from up ahead. A patrol possibly. Amilkar crouched deeper into the shadows, making himself totally invisible to whoever or whatever was approaching down the street. He could hear a shuffling along the stones, getting closer. If he was spotted, it would be his end.

In the light of the few torches still burning, Amilkar breathed in sudden relief. It was a single horned soldier, carrying a torch as he walked sleepily through the streets, on his appointed rounds. Immediately, the assassin could see one of the things he required. A hooded cape which hung off the soldier's armour. His muscles tensed slightly as he prepared himself to move, watching the soldier's movements closely. He knew he would have to be precise, silent, and very quick. His training would make it easy for him to overcome this lone soldier, as long as he was careful not to make too much noise.

"Death from the shadows." His master's instruction leapt into his thoughts, as his yellow eyes gazed upon his unsuspecting prey, approaching. In the darkness, he slowed his breathing, watching every movement, his hearing acutely tuned in to any sound. Other than this creature's clumsy, tired footsteps, the only noise was the night song of desert insects. He had no weapon, but for this, he would not need one.

He waited until the horned soldier was three steps past where he was hidden, and launched himself out of the darkness. Fast and silent, he took the soldier from behind without a sound, his weight, and velocity knocking his victim to the far side of the street next to the well. He quickly disarmed the reptile, taking his sword and reversing it on him like lightning. The soldier was dead almost instantly, not even having the time to inhale, to scream. Amilkar pulled the sword quickly from his prey's flesh, swinging it at the torch on the wall in a very measured motion. The lit end of the torch was severed, toppling off the fixture it was held in, falling into the depths of the well. All was dark and silent once again, and Amilkar became as motionless as stone. He waited, listening and watching to determine whether or not the commotion would raise an alarm. Nothing.

He slowly dragged the body of the soldier into the darkness beside the well, rifling through his belongings. He now had the cape, which would protect him from the heat of the desert sun, and although he wasn't worried as much about weapons, he slid the sword belt around his own waist. There was also a water skin, made of leather, which he filled by pulling up the bucket from the well. Now, the only thing preventing him from freedom were the walls of the city itself.

Amilkar already felt more at ease, eager to escape to the sands outside of Stigia. Once there, he knew his training would keep him concealed until he reached safety. He untied the bucket, placing it silently out of sight behind the well, and rolled up the rope. He would need it. Looking up and down the street once more to be sure it was clear, he jetted back across the cobblestone, putting his back to the outside wall of the city. He moved along in the deepest of the darkness, moving behind several buildings on his way toward the first available stairs that would take him to the top of the wall. He would have to use extreme caution, as there would likely be more guards.

The air was cool and still, there was no wind to mask any sound he would have made. Still, he was not worried. The monitor was completely silent as he moved swiftly along the wall, coming to a halt behind a tall stone tower which rose high above the cobblestone street. It was a guard tower, where the Stigian archers could see out over the walls of the city, in case it was attacked.

Amilkar could only ever remember one story about any kind of assault on Stigia, and it did not work out well for the enemies of the Empire. Their siege attempt had been futile. The Stigian hordes had poured out of the city to pursue the would-be attackers as their lines had broken, scattering the remainder of their armies to the winds.

He stopped, watching the top of the wall above him. Around the other side of the tower, there were stairs, wrapping against the stone lookout's side, connecting the street to the ramparts up above. He surveyed everything. He could see the sides of the keep as well, and scanned the windows, which were completely dark now.

Waiting for what he thought was the perfect moment, he moved quickly around the tower, ascending the stone steps silently. At the top, he tucked himself back into the darkness of the tower. It was not a moment too soon, as a guard emerged from the top of the gatehouse not far away down the wall. Amilkar paused, melting into the darkness. His yellow eyes watched the approaching soldier carefully, his breath calm and steady. He slid the sword at his hip out of its scabbard without a sound. If the horned reptile kept on his present course, he would come face to face with the hidden assassin.

Just as Amilkar prepared himself to attack the guard first, the lizard turned abruptly, heading down the stairs that the monitor had just come up. The assassin exhaled deeply, putting the sword away. With the coast now clear, he wasted no time. Tying the rope around one of the ramparts beside him, he leapt over the wall, repelling down the tall stones to the sand below. With a full water skin and all the necessary supplies he needed, Amilkar sprinted away from the wall into the darkness of the desert dunes. He did not even glance back behind him, knowing that the Stigian soldiers, even if they did spot him, would not follow him into the Sand Sea at night.

~~~~~

The darkness of nightfall had turned the deep green of the jungle undergrowth into blackness and shadow. The companions crept through the rainforest greenery, trying desperately to keep moving despite their exhaustion. Chase knew that they had to find this secret place as quickly as possible, as they practically stumbled through the underbrush. There would
~~~~~

be others looking for it by now. He would not be surprised to run into a patrol of scouts from Stigia at any moment. Surely Cyrus was looking for this artifact as well, seeing as he had not yet mounted another attack on the races of the rainforest in another attempt to recover the Gecko's Gate. It made sense to him. It also worried him all the same, as he had no real desire to face off against more of Cyrus' horned soldiers.

He stopped, listening.

"Don't get separated!" he exclaimed through the gloom of the jungle surrounding him. "Keep saying something every once in a while so we don't lose each other."

The others said a brief greeting, and Chase could tell by listening that Jonas was the furthest away. He breathed a sigh of relief after another moment as the undergrowth stirred, and Jonas spoke again, much closer now. He heard another sound as well, a distant hum which he thought was somehow familiar. It grew louder now, and after several moments, began to fade away again. It came from above the canopy of the forest. Something had just flown over top of them. Perhaps someone or something was searching for them. Chase hoped that it was simply some kind of large insect, out on a night hunt. He could hear his pulse beating in his ears, and he tightened his grip on the hilt of his sword in the humid darkness. This part of the forest was a deep place in the jungle that he had never visited before, and it made him a little uneasy. Chase felt totally lost now, although he had said nothing to the others. They looked at him with their usual confidence, and he did not wish to startle them by being indecisive or confused. They had moved through the rainforest in what he thought may have been circles now that he did not have the sun penetrating the canopy to guide him. The stars had been mostly hidden by the thick growth and vines, as the leaves here grew larger than twice the size of dinner plates. Without a solid way to know which direction they were headed, Chase had defaulted to his best guess, which was definitely not the way he liked to do things.

As if on cue, Kiko finally asked the question that he had not wanted to answer.

"Are you sure we are heading west?" she inquired quietly from somewhere in the gloom.

"Yeah, I'm pretty sure." he replied quickly.

There was silence for a moment, and Chase hoped that it would be the end of the questions.

"It doesn't sound like you are too sure to me!" she stated.

Chase was glad that she could not see him roll his eyes in the darkness.

"And don't bother rolling your eyes at me, either." she followed.

Jonas chuckled lightly.

Chase could hear movement in the brush, heavy and slow, coming closer to him. It was Dantis, he was sure by the careless snapping of twigs and the sound of sheer bulk in the brush. Chase held out a scaled hand in the dark, stopping Dantis before the large chameleon stepped on him.

"Sorry. Couldn't see ya." Dantis said quietly.

"No kidding." Chase replied with a trace of sarcasm.

It was getting ridiculous to continue this way, and Chase knew it. It wasn't as if they could move silently in this kind of thick growth. He reached into his pack, withdrawing a cloth and a small bottle of oil. Grabbing a nearby branch, he broke it off to a length of about two feet. He wrapped the cloth around one end, and poured the oil on it, soaking the cloth well.

"Give me your Flint, Dantis." said Chase.

Without a reply, Dantis removed his own pack, and after a few seconds of fumbling around in it, placed a piece of bent metal with two stones clasped in it in Chase's hand. Chase struck it several times near the crude construction he held, and the oil lit finally, sputtering to life, until a warm glowing flame lit the rainforest around him. Kiko and Jonas emerged, drawn to the light of the torch.

"Well, which way do we go, boss?" asked Jonas with a slight grin.

"Yeah. Thought you knew where to go!" said Kiko.

Chase exhaled deeply in frustration, beginning to become a bit agitated.

"Have any of you ever been to the Grove of Light before?" he asked.

The shaking of their scaled heads and the shrug of shoulders was all he needed.

"Then shut it. I need to be able to see the stars to find out where we are." he continued hotly.

"Sorry." replied Jonas, taken aback slightly.

Kiko looked equally stung.

"Maybe one of you can hold this while I climb to the canopy and try to get a look at the sky?" Chase continued, thrusting the torch to Dantis.

The gecko did not wait to get a reply, instead jumping up onto the trunk of a very large tree nearby. Dantis held the torch high in an effort to light as much of the way as possible. Jonas and Kilo quickly forgot their friend's ill-tempered words as they watched him climb deftly up the massive tree by the light of the torch.

Chase climbed carefully as the light diminished. He was at a dizzying height now, and kept his eyes focused on the patches of sky he could see through the leaves above. A few minutes later, he poked his scaled face out through the top of the canopy, bathed now in the light reflected off the giant rings surrounding their world. The silver light shone down upon the tops of the leaves of the rainforest, and for a moment, all that Chase could do was stare out across the sea of trees, washed in the beauty of celestial light.

He scanned the skies.

"Well, what do you see up there?" called Kiko from the forest floor.

Chase looked down through the leaves, almost like submerging his head underwater.

"You guys have to see this...!" he shouted down at them.

It didn't take long, and the others gradually made their way up to where Chase sat in the crook of a high branch. They each found a spot to raise their heads above the foliage to take in the view.

Kiko gasped as she saw the landscape unfolded before her, stretching endlessly in the light of the night sky. Jonas and Dantis were speechless.

After a minute that seemed stretched, Kiko finally broke the sublime silence.

"So, uh... where do we go from here? Chase, do you know where we are?" she asked, still mesmerized by the sight in front of her.

Chase simply pointed over the treetops, slightly to their right. There seemed to be a dim glow emanating from within the trees some distance away. It outshone the light from the skies above. It was just bright enough to stand out from the rest of the rainforest canopy, but too bright to be cast by firelight from an enemy camp. It had to be the Glowing Grove.

~~~~~

Horned lizards scurried about madly in the keep of Stigia, seeing to the last small details of a banquet to mark the arrival of the ruling family from the nomads of Nostria. The monitors were set to arrive that very evening, and the Emperor would be host to the family of his soon to be bride. Not one of the reptiles hurrying to perform their appointed tasks wanted to upset the Emperor by failing to create perfection for the feast that evening.

Floors were mopped and mopped again. The stoneware was polished. A virtual army of cooks and servers bustled in and out of the massive kitchen
~~~~~

in the keep, perfecting delectable dishes of insects, dried beetles, and seaweed salads. Some of the ingredients had come from lands far away, rushed to Stigia through the blinding Sand Sea to ensure their freshness was kept intact.

Outside the keep, the wall guards were doubled, and Cyrus' personal Imperial guards were dressed in their best uniforms, copper spears and shields polished to a high sheen. Even the city streets seemed clean, swept by many of the peasant inhabitants of Stigia. If the residents wanted to eat, they had to work for the food, supplied and controlled by the Empire. Water was even more precious here in the middle of the desert, and the army was supplied with a great deal more than normal citizens.

Everyone in Stigia was busy this day with a task of some kind. Soldiers roamed the streets with whips, ready to punish any reptile that was not working hard. Every lizard in Stigia knew well what the fuss was all about. This would be the first Emperor to take a wife as far back as anyone could remember, a fact that created whispers and rumours in the streets day and night since it had been announced.

Up in the throne room, Cyrus sat brooding while several horned lizard servants fussed over his attire. He was dressed in a large formal black cape, with a red interior, and bands of gold surrounded his copper armour. Even the scabbard of his sword had been redone with matching gold banding.

"Please hold still for just one more moment, Your Grace." said one the servants adjusting his cape.

The only reason Cyrus complied silently was the fact that the servant was a female, and it was a bit early in the day to be killing any of the servants. He finally growled at his subjects, indicating that he wished to be left alone for a moment. They bowed quickly, exiting the throne room to avoid angering the Emperor. Only his guards remained, standing at attention, stoic and silent.

Cyrus sighed heavily, rubbing clawed hands across his scaled forehead. He found this preparation nonsense irritating and useless. The only thing he relished preparing for was battle. He had questioned whether or not he had made the right decision for weeks now, and with the leaders of Nostria arriving this evening, he could feel the pressure on him building. As he pondered the strategic advantages that Nostria's inclusion in the Empire would bring, it eased his mind. He would have legions of the monitors which made up their race, all with the basic training of the assassins that had made the reptiles of the northern badlands so infamous. It would also bring him another group of highly adept assassins, after the loss of his last trusted entourage. Leaving

Amilkar alive had obviously been a mistake, as he had not found a willing commander in the female gecko, her talent at battle notwithstanding. This part of the equation made him feel like he had personally failed himself, and the realm he was meant to rule. It had frustrated and enraged him that she would not accept the great honour he had been ready to bestow upon her. Her escape, along with the remaining assassin, was the final straw. He would send troops to find them both and destroy them once and for all. It would be necessary for him to deploy a division of his soldiers now anyway, for more than one purpose. He needed to deal with Alibesh and Amilkar, and he needed to find this strange artifact in the grove of light, hidden deep within the rainforest.

He had to assume that the Chameleon King was searching for it as well, and that The Three were probably also involved. Just thinking of the three young reptiles caused the blood to rise in his eyes, made him grit his teeth slightly and clench a scaled fist. They would not succeed ahead of him this time. He had to crush them finally and be rid of their meddling forever. They had destroyed his ambitions several times now, and he would not allow them to continue to be a threat to his vision of conquest for the Empire. His plans had been ruined by these young misfits enough. It would not happen again. He had to find this 'Glowing Grove', and discover the secret of the weapon hidden there.

His thoughts were interrupted as a short, horned lizard dressed in the robes of one of his royal advisors walked through the large wooden doors of the throne room. He slowed his walk as he approached the raised platform where the Emperor sat on his black throne. He bowed toward Cyrus, deeply. His schooling in etiquette and proper conduct in the upper houses of the Empire had gone on for the last three reptiles to sit on the throne of Stigia. Despite his own ideas of what should come of this world, Cyrus respected this lizard, and trusted his council. His name was Vitos. He straightened again, his arms folded beneath his robes, awaiting the Emperor's word to speak. He was well schooled in etiquette and was too old to fear anything that might be considered punishment if he were to say more than he should.

Cyrus nodded to him, returning the old lizard's cordial approach. He straightened on the throne, raising a scaled hand toward him in an indication that he was awaiting what he had to say.

"Your Grace, the caravan from Nostria has been spotted approaching from the north. It might be prudent to send a welcoming party to escort them into the city gates." he said.

Cyrus contemplated this for a moment. Showing good manners would indeed ease this event forward without problems. He did not want the monitors from the north to think of the Empire as weak, or without education. Stigia would always be seen as the capital of Evaria, thought Cyrus, despite his rough and bloody warlord beginnings.

"Very well, let us dispatch a small contingent of the Royal Guard to meet them for escort." the Emperor affirmed.

Vitos bowed once again in acknowledgment of the command, turning without further hesitation to carry out the instructions. His robes flowed across the polished black onyx of the throne room floors on his way back toward the doors, and he held his short, stocky body straight as he neared the entrance to the throne room.

"One last thing Vitos." commanded the Emperor.

The old lizard stopped at the doors, obediently turning back toward Cyrus.

The Emperor leaned forward on the dark wood of the throne, resting his scaled elbows on the armrests of the ancient furniture, his yellow eyes focused on the horned lizard at the doors.

"Have the historians bring me every map, every parchment, every scrap of information from the archives that has anything to do with the uncharted areas of the rainforests to the south..."

10

The Sand Sea stretched out before her to the horizon as Alibesh held the reins of her wasp mount loosely, crouching slightly in the saddle. The horned soldiers from Stigia were still behind her, keeping up, but not really gaining any ground on her. She had perhaps taken the wasp out of the group in the stables which was the strongest, strictly out of pure luck. She would have to do something about her pursuers before long, especially before deciding on a final course. If one of them happened to escape, they would report her direction of travel, and more soldiers would eventually be in pursuit of her.

The gecko let the wasp do what it was meant to, guiding it low over the hot sand. She sped along, looking for anything punctuating the endless dunes that might give her an advantage of some kind. She lowered herself further on the wasp's back, trying to cut any wind resistance her scaled body might create, becoming one with her mount. Alibesh hoped that she could put at least a little more distance between herself and the soldiers in pursuit, to perhaps allow her time to formulate a plan to deal with them. The hot, dry air blew against her as the wasp raced across the desert. She shielded her eyes against the sun with a scaled hand, looking toward the horizon. The sand dunes stretched on forever, but she could see a dark line beginning to form where the distant land met the sky. It had to be the rainforests.

She now knew exactly what she must do, gripping the reins of the wasp a bit tighter. Alibesh guided her ride lower over the sands of the desert, the rapid pulse of its wings stirring up a trail of dust behind them. It would make it easier for her pursuers to follow. Despite the desperate situation she was in, a slight grin traced her reptilian lips as a plan formed in her mind. She would rid herself of these vermin, and they would die much deserved deaths. The female gecko preferred a straight on fight instead of running away. Although she had no weapon with her, she was confident that she could overcome these simple soldiers who were chasing her. It was a dumb move, to give up the only weapon she had leaving the arena, she knew. But it had shed weight, and allowed her to keep both hands on the reins of her mount.

More importantly, that small amount of weight kept her ahead of the heavier, armour clad soldiers who followed behind. She wasn't really worried. She would find a replacement weapon. One of theirs, once she had dispatched them. She had made her masters and her village a great deal of wealth fighting in the arena. And three horned soldiers from the desert empire would be no match for her if she were to arm herself with even a crude weapon of some kind. What concerned her was the idea that if she was unable to kill them all, that the rest of Stigia would know where she was…

The line of trees began to look thicker on the horizon as Alibesh and her wasp sped along above the hot sands. She cast another glance back over her shoulder, and could see the three horned soldiers following behind, fighting to stay out of the large dust trail her mount was raising from the desert floor. She grinned. They would follow her exact path, and the female gecko looked forward again, toward the wall of greenery coming at her ever more quickly. A plan was beginning to form in her reptilian mind. She had no weapons, and yet the forest growing larger in front of her could easily provide a means to rid herself of the reptiles chasing her. She would need to be quick, and have a little bit of luck, but she could do this, and live to fight another day. The beast in her soul was not nearly ready to give up yet.

The individual trees were becoming visible now, as she kicked her heels into the wasp's sides to spur it on. She needed enough room between herself and the soldiers behind her to maneuver. The sands below had become punctuated by the occasional low palmetto and scrub grass at the edge of the arid desert approached. Her fate was coming straight at her as well, although she was unaware of it.

She brought the wasp ever lower, practically skimming the surface of the hot sands. The creature responded instantly to her commands, dodging between stands of palmetto as she scanned her rapidly passing surroundings for anything she could use.

The wall of ancient trees forming the perimeter of the rainforests now towered above the desert, the shade and cool within the depths of its vast canopy beckoning to Alibesh as she sped forward. Out of the corner of her eye, she spotted something which would help her. Arching her ride hard to the left, she circled around low, to get a better look. The soldiers following her struggled to make the highspeed turn, barely staying with her.

The female gecko had spied just the thing she was looking for. She leaned to her side as they approached a stand of dead wood, tall straight spikes, remains of trees which had not survived on the harsh edge of the desert. In a flash, she reached out as the wasp sped past. She winced in pain as the force of the breaking piece of tree wrenched her shoulder. But it came free as she righted herself again in the saddle of the wasp, her new weapon firmly in her grip. Alibesh levelled the long, thick piece of wood forward, turning her mount again, this time cutting hard back toward the horned reptiles who were in pursuit.

She had a perfect lance made of wood, pointed forward as she sped toward the Stigian soldiers. She targeted the lead wasp, setting herself rigidly forward in the saddle, locking the wood against her side firmly. The horned soldier's eyes grew wide as he realized what she intended to do, and fumbled to pull his sword from its scabbard. He had run out of time, and as Alibesh raced between the soldiers in mid-air, her lance caught the lead soldier directly in the middle of his copper body armour. He flew off of his mount, landing in the sand thirty feet below in a heap of bloodied scales and copper. The wasp continued past, without a rider to guide it, slowing, confused.

Alibesh leaned away as she flew past the two remaining soldiers, avoiding their drawn sword blades easily. Her mount however, was not so lucky. The slice of a sword cleanly removed a large piece of one of its wings. Together, the female gecko and her wasp pitched to the side, almost throwing her off. She held onto the reins, guiding the wasp down to a rough landing in the sand next to a large palmetto. Alibesh was thrown out of the saddle into the sand as her ride crashed in a cloud of sand and dust. She picked herself up out of the coarse dune, small rivers of sand running off her scaled body.

Her makeshift lance had shattered on her first target, so she was once again without a weapon. She shook off the fog in her head from the impact, looking around quickly for the remaining two reptiles chasing her. They were still a fair way away, just beginning to turn their wasps back around to come back. Alibesh wasted no time, launching herself out of the sand toward the fallen Stigian soldier that she had bested earlier. He was not far away, and she reached him quickly, tearing the scabbard and belt from around his crumpled body, and throwing it over her shoulder. Steel sang as she withdrew the sword from its sheath, turning and sprinting toward the line of the rainforest trees not far away.

It was far from over, as she could hear the thrum of the wasp's wings behind her growing louder. She did not look back, running hard through the patchy groups of palmetto toward the shade of the forest. She raised the blade of the sword, levelling it above her head to catch the sun's rays. She angled the steel to where she thought the wasp's position might be, hoping her desperate plan would work. The sound of their wings became almost deafening as she broke through the first line of tall trees, jumping over fallen logs and low undergrowth with lungs that were on fire from exertion. Just as Alibesh sprinted into the shade of the canopy, the sun caught the blade of her sword, blinding her two pursuers momentarily. They pulled back on their mounts, for fear of crashing into the trees. It had bought her the seconds she needed to stay out of their grasp.

The female gecko stopped briefly, breathing heavily, and glanced back to the desert sands outside the canopy which now covered her in cool shade. The two Stigian soldiers had landed their wasps, and were struggling to dismount to follow her into the rainforest. A grin graced her scaled face, and she let them see her sheath the blade of the sword, gesturing for them to follow. This seemed to enrage them, and they stumbled into the shade of the trees in pursuit of her again. To give up the chase and return to Stigia now would be suicide for them, and they knew it.

She turned away, easily dodging through the thickening jungle as the sun sank lower in the sky. The grin remained on her face, her eyes adjusting to the deeply shaded forest. It was much cooler here, and Alibesh could already feel the humidity of the jungle soothing her scales through her torn tunic. They had chased her to the wrong place. This was a place where the advantage was *hers…*

~~~~~

Yami sat patiently while the other female monitors fussed over her appearance. It was difficult for them, she knew, trying to prepare her for their arrival in Stigia in a large covered carriage which occasionally bounced over the desert sands. Her assistants, Maily and Yokady, worked to get the princess of Nostria dressed properly to meet with her soon-to-be husband, the Emperor of Stigia.

Yami was seated amongst a small sea of earth-toned fabric pillows in the center of the large floor of the carriage, tired of the voyage toward Stigia after two days of travel. She sincerely hoped that they would see the city by the end of this day, if for no other reason than to change the boring Sand Sea landscape. Her lightweight dress of beige fabric was draped perfectly around her, her assistants dressed in the same colours, but much more simple attire.

The entire idea still had Yami upset. She did not like or approve of this
~~~~~

wedding. She knew that it was customary to be betrothed to another in Nostria, but to be wed to a uromastyx from the desert was simply unacceptable. Everything she knew about this reptile, which was not very much indeed, told her that this was a bad idea, regardless of her father's political ambitions with Stigia. On top of everything else, she would have to live here in the desert, far away from the world that she was used to. As a princess of Nostria, she had everything done for her, for the most part. She did not have to seek out food or water. It was brought to her. She did not have to hunt or cook or clean. It was done for her.

Yami was certain of another thing. She would be there to simply look beautiful, and be dressed up, but she would have little or no real power or decision-making privileges. This arrangement of becoming the first new Empress of Stigia in many years would only benefit Cyrus Malthor and her father.

The carriage was large and comfortable, well-appointed with pillows and silk covering the windows to shade the interior from the desert heat. It was hauled across the Sand Sea by huge beetles, strapped with bridles and reins, guided by a sole driver aboard the large enclosed house at the front of the carriage. It was more like some sort of sand barge than a carriage, except that it had numerous wood wheels with wide treads to assist it across the dunes. It had been constructed in the badlands of Nostria as a transport for the ruling family, with no expense spared on its lavish comforts. In addition to the grand carriage, there were several smaller supply wagons, carrying gifts and food for the wedding.

The entourage was escorted by many monitors from the various assassin's guilds of Nostria, most were assembled and on foot, with a dozen or more mounted on giant beetles. The beasts were tireless and strong, rarely needing food or water to continue the journey, and the Nostrians had always valued them as a great asset when traveling.

Yami turned and watched through the veil over the carriage windows, seeing the desert dunes passing slowly by. Even out of the sun, the heat was sweltering, and the air dry. The young Nostrian princess could only imagine the discomfort of the carriage drivers, and the rest of their entourage outside were dealing with, despite wearing sheer fabric cloaks and head wraps to keep the scorching sun at bay.

As if sensing her thoughts, Maily and Yokady hurried forward with wet cloths, and began to wipe down the princess' exposed scales on her arms and face, in an attempt to keep her dark reptilian skin from cracking or peeling. Their primary concern was to deliver the princess to Stigia in perfect, beautiful condition for her wedding. The two female monitors checked the princess' scales to feel how heated Yami was, and Yokady clapped her hands together quickly.

Yet another monitor arrived quickly, carrying a large fan made of the feathers of a giant hawk. She seated herself just behind Yami, slowly fanning her in an attempt to provide some cool breeze for the bride. She was dressed the very same as Maily and Yokady, who continued to dampen the princess' scaled skin.

"Thank you, Joa." Yami said.

The young female did not reply and remained intently focused on her task.

The princess turned her attention back to the windows, as the massive wheels of the carriage crept across the desert sands. The trip from the badlands in the north had taken forever, it seemed, and Yami could only hope that it would soon be over. She had only ever been to Stigia once, when she was just a hatchling, and remembered little of it. Her thoughts became dark as she remembered that this time, she would not be leaving Stigia. The monitor wondered if she would ever see her homeland in the Nostrian wastes again. Perhaps on few and far between diplomatic trips sometime in the future. She reminded herself to press her father to speak to the Emperor about such things, so that she might have some diplomatic privileges. Without any of it, she would be sentenced to being little more than a fixture in Stigia, with no official position or responsibilities. It would be a very boring existence.

On cue, a door at the front of the carriage opened, and Yami's father stepped in. Tall and thin, he approached the young females, waving his daughter's servants away. They departed quickly, with a bow to the tall reptile standing before them.

His name was Taran, and he was the Lord of Nostria. He was the Nomad ruler of the badlands, as well as the overseer of the assassin's guild. He wore the same thin cloak as the others in the caravan along with a large head wrap that also covered most of his scaled face for protection from the sun and blowing sand.

He removed it now, exposing a face both old and wise in appearance. Despite the hardships of nomadic life in Nostria, and the ruthless training of the assassins, there was a slight softness in the Lord's yellow eyes.

Taran had ruled Nostria in a very different way than Stigia. He believed in balance, both in the lives of the inhabitants of his kingdom, and the diversity of the races of all of Evaria. He respected the Emperor of Stigia, but he also respected the Chameleon King. His allegiances were somewhere in between, favouring neither of them, favouring his own subjects above all of the rest. If Cyrus Malthor or Maxxus were to fall in battle, it meant nothing to Taran. Some other reptile would succeed them, and things would not change much in the end. Evaria would go on. He had only agreed to these ties to Stigia to secure a more prosperous future for his race. Whether or not the Emperor succeeded in his mission of conquest was inconsequential to him.

"I know you are weary of travel, my dear, but we will arrive soon enough." Taran said to his daughter, seated comfortably amongst the pillows in front of him.

"Yes, Father. I am sure we will." she replied simply.

Yami knew she was doing a terrible job of concealing her lack of enthusiasm regarding the whole thing. She did not wish to offend or upset her father, and she knew that he was aware that she did not approve of the wedding, or Stigia for that matter. The princess knew as well that none of it mattered. Her father viewed it as her duty, in the end.

The door in the front of the room opened again, and another monitor poked his wrapped head into the room.

"Pardon, my Lord, but there is a contingent of Royal Guardsmen from Stigia approaching from up ahead." he announced.

"That would be our escort, I would imagine..." Taran replied.

The princess rose from her seat amongst the pillows, stepping forward to join her father as he followed the other monitor back out of the door. She was anxious to see something other than sand dunes, even if she was not enthralled with the idea of what the escort represented.

The sun was high in the sky, making all shadows short against the Sand Sea. The heat was intense, and the air was so dry that she could feel the moisture leaving her body just standing in the sun. Standing on the front deck of the massive carriage, Yami shielded her eyes against the blinding radiance of the seemingly endless sands. The huge beetles pulled them all forward, flanked by riders on Iguanas and the other smaller supply carriages. On the crest of a dune directly in front of the caravan, she could see the copper armour and shields worn by Stigian Imperial Guards. They flew crimson banners with the symbols of the Empire on them.

Yami sighed heavily. It was her destiny approaching. Her destiny was to become the Empress...

<div align="center">~~~~~</div>

Chase was barely able to catch the movement out of the corner of his eye, before cold steel appeared out of the thick greenery next to his scaled throat.

"Do not make a sound, or it will be your last..." a female voice whispered close behind him.

Chase flushed slightly. How had he been out-maneuvered, and taken by surprise in the rainforests he hunted so successfully in?

He had no choice but to be still and remain silent, as the horned soldiers tramped through the forest, searching. It dawned on him that they were not looking for he and his friends, but were in fact on the hunt for the reptile who now held a dagger to his throat. He remained motionless in the shrubbery, his eyes following the soldiers into the clearing they had just been in minutes ago. This was a strange situation indeed, he thought to himself. In quickly hiding from the approaching soldiers from Stigia, they had somehow wound up in the same thick jungle growth which hid their true quarry, and without even noticing her. Chase was now obviously certain that whatever the creature was holding the knife to him, it was a she. It was a good thing she was so friendly, or he would have been dead by now was his next sarcastic thought in silence.

The two soldiers spoke to one another in low tones as they looked around the forest clearing, and although Chase could not make out everything they were saying, he knew that they were becoming agitated. Their prey had eluded them, and it would soon be total darkness in the rainforest. Chase could only hope that they would not elect to make camp right here in the clearing for the coming night. He could feel the cold edge of the dagger against the scales of his neck. If they did, it could be a very long night...

But eventually they disappeared further into the jungle, quietly bickering with one another as to how stupid the other one was, and Chase carefully exhaled. Still, his assailant didn't remove the blade. Dantis had silently crept forward a half step beside Chase.

"I would not move any further, my big friend, or the gecko here might suddenly not be able to speak or breathe ever again." the voice behind Chase hissed in the shadows.

"Let him go." whispered Kiko, her bowstring drawn with an arrow notched. She had ever so slowly moved her aim from the soldiers to the space

~98~

behind Chase filled with vines and leaves.

"You sure you have me in your aim?" Chuckled the female voice quietly. "It would be a pity for you to miss me, your friend might lose something very important to him."

Kiko blushed in anger as she listened to the voice, and realized that she could not really see her, whoever she was. She could have been aiming at space filled by nothing but plants.

For long minutes, they sat in their stalemate amongst the shrubbery, no one moving. The only sound was the chorus of the insect songs in the undergrowth, as night's darkness grew deeper. Finally, another voice broke the quiet.

"You had best remove your little knife from my pal's throat, or you might lose something as well...your life!"

It was Jonas. Somewhere behind Chase, and seemingly, behind his stealthy attacker as well. The male gecko had managed to out-flank this invisible threat. The blade slowly withdrew from Chase's neck.

There came a quick sound in the dark, like a fork stuck suddenly in a vegetable, and a small yelp in a female voice. There was a commotion as a reptile form launched out of the shrubbery. The sound of steel singing from a scabbard could be heard, and the friends all held their weapons forward in defense, their eyes on the silhouette of a reptile holding both a sword and a dagger in the deepening gloom.

"Come forward and you shall have a quick death!" said the female voice.

The companions did not move from their places in the shrubbery, weapons ready.

Chase whispered to Jonas.

"What was that all about?"

Jonas hesitated in the darkness. Then the words seemed to spill out of him uncontrollably.

"I wanted her to get away from you, so I gave her a little poke with my sword!" he said.

Chase tried to stifle a laugh, despite the seriousness of their situation.

"We are not your enemy, but those soldiers are!" replied Kiko, now aimed dead on with her bow.

"Once I kill you, I will deal with the horned ones as well!" the figure in the dark exclaimed.

Dantis spoke up.

"Or, you keep making noise and we will end up tying you to a tree for your little horned friends to find you..." he said firmly.

"Who are you?" asked Chase. "And why are you so eager to kill us when you know nothing about us?"

The silhouette did not answer, but the friends could tell that she relaxed her guard a bit, lowering her weapons to her side. They, in turn, relaxed slightly.

"My apologies, but I have been continuously attacked since I escaped the desert, and I have not been able to rest in days of being pursued..." she said, losing some of the edge in her voice. What remained sounded hollow, exhausted.

The companions slowly emerged from the shrubbery, still cautious of the shadowy figure that they could not identify. There was something familiar about this reptile none the less. Chase especially could not understand why, but the female lizard here in the rainforest clearing was definitely not like the horned soldiers the friends had hidden so quickly from.

They stood deadlocked again for a few moments.

"You gonna put those weapons away, or do we all need to hug first?" asked Dantis sarcastically.

Even in the gloom, Chase could sense the female reptile's irritation, as he heard her scoff slightly at the chameleon's words. Regardless, she slowly slid the sword back into a scabbard she had quickly slung over her hips, the dagger disappearing inside of a torn tunic she wore.

The companions relaxed, putting away their own weapons. Only Kiko stayed where she was, keeping her bow trained on the mysterious guest.

"Kiko, put your bow away, she means us no harm." Chase said quietly.

"I didn't hear those words from her..." replied Kiko, ignoring the request.

Chase began to quickly become aggravated, considering Kiko's sudden defiance as simply rude in the face of the eased tension. The female anole still had the stranger locked in her sights.

"Kiko! Put it away!" exclaimed Chase angrily.

"Yeah, c'mon! Let's not make things worse!" affirmed Jonas.

Kiko hesitated another few moments, finally lowering her bow slowly. She could feel the other creature's eyes on her, calculating and cold, even though she could not see the details of her face very well in the darkness of the undergrowth.

"Thanks for deciding against me killing you, anole..." the creature hissed sarcastically.

Chase ignored the nasty comment, despite the fact that he knew that Kiko's face was undoubtedly flushed with anger at the moment. He was now curious about this reptile.

"Who are you, and why are you here? And why are soldiers from Stigia looking for you?" he asked.

"You always ask this many questions when you first meet a female in the rainforest?" she asked in return.

Chase was glad that the darkness hid the blushing he could suddenly feel in his reptilian cheeks. The stranger waited a moment or two before responding, perhaps wondering if she should tell these lizards anything at all.

"My name is Alibesh. I am from the village of Sedda on the high plains." she began cautiously.

"So you are a skink?" asked Dantis.

After another pause, the female reptile responded.

"Not really."

"And the horned soldiers looking for you?" chimed Kiko.

"I escaped from the Stigian dungeons, and was pursued here. It was the first place that I could evade them beyond the desert." she replied.

There was a spark, and the friends shielded their eyes against a sudden, painfully bright light. The stranger had struck a flint to a torch she held above her, to expose who the reptiles around her actually were, and what they looked like.

As their eyes adjusted, the friends gasped slightly, looking at the female reptile standing in the small clearing in front of them. She was a gecko, just like Chase and Jonas. Her scales had more black over her body than they did, but she was a gecko none the less. To Chase, she was beautiful to behold. She had an air of danger about her as well, the sight her dark scales giving him a slight chill, despite the heat and humidity of the jungle. He could feel his heart speed up in his chest, could feel the rush of hot blood to his face.

"You are a gecko, and you don't come from Andar, but from the plains?" he asked.

She brought her large vertically slit eyes to rest directly on his as she spoke.

"As I said before, you ask a lot of questions..."

11

A lone horned soldier sat at a stone desk in one of the rooms of the keep, the hot desert sun streaming in the small window beside him...

He was writing orders for the main legion of troops, whose responsibility it was to provide watch and defense on the city's outer wall.

His name was Aryan, and he had recently been promoted to Commander of the Stigian armies by the Emperor himself. It was the way in which he had followed all orders perfectly and imposed strict discipline on any of the troops who had not done the same that had impressed his leader. He had improved the efficiency of changes in the watch, and had increased new conscriptions since taking his new position with ice cold precision.

Aryan had taken a very personal interest in improving the army's training regimen, doubling the amount of time spent with swordplay and tactics, and creating specialized small units with various abilities. It had been a laborious process, but in the end, he had begun to mold his troops to the way he saw them being at their best.

He was tall for a horned lizard, which also helped maintain the respect of the army under his command, along with the strict, icy way he dealt with any issue which might arise. He sat, composing the daily orders with a quill and ink, including his instructions for each of the many units on separate sheets of parchment. As he completed each one, he would stamp it with his own unique seal, one of the many ways he secured his communications. No soldier was to interpret orders they received as authentic unless they bore his seal.

The room he was in served as both office and his personal quarters, simple and neat, with only a few essentials he required. His bed was nothing more than a raised stone slab with a neatly folded blanket and rolled cloth for a pillow. There were a few shelves on the opposite wall which held his clothing and uniforms, with a few rock knobs to hang his cape and sword belt on.

His amenities were simple, but his mind, at the same time, was the opposite. His thought processes analyzed everything around him, seen and unseen. He used a great deal more than his existing senses, and specialized in knowing all that was happening in Stigia. From the citizens to the military forces, from the youngest poor hatchling, to the eldest street vendor, Aryan knew everything that happened in the city, using the reports from his patrols, along with his own casual strolls through the cobblestone streets. Nothing escaped his attention.

It was these things which had been noticed by the Emperor, allowing him to rise quickly to the position he now held. It suited him well, as the garrison of the city, to say nothing of the bulk of the Stigian forces, had never been in better condition. It was a matter of pride to Aryan.

There was a quiet rap at the wooden door to his chamber, and the commander grunted a brief word for the unseen caller to enter. The soldier who came through the door was the captain of the wall guard, and he stepped to the edge of the stone desk quickly, uttering his report to Aryan quickly and to the point. The commander listened intently, though he did not look up from his writing. As the captain finished speaking, Aryan nodded slowly. Finishing the page of parchment he was working on, he quickly stamped it with his seal, and handed it directly to the soldier in front of him.

"Thank you," he began without a trace of true gratitude or change in his expression. "Here are the orders for the Nostrian's arrival…"

He finally looked up at the captain as he handed over the paper, his eyes ice cold.

"Please ensure that the watch continues properly, even after our visitors arrive, and that all security measures are in place." he added.

The horned soldier snapped a cordial nod, retrieving the parchment, and stepping quickly back out the door. As it closed behind him, the commander turned his attention toward the small window in the room, taking a quick break with his own thoughts. Outside, the city streets were busy, every reptile going about the work of tidying the city for the arrival of the guests from the badlands to the north.

Aryan did not like the idea of this visit at all. He knew the Emperor's plans, but also acknowledged the fact that this coming commotion would tax his ability to keep the city's defenses tight and without compromise.

He rested his chin in his scaly hands for a moment, content to watch the activity in the heat of the desert sun outside the window. He knew that he would have to be focused during the next few days, with an eye on every detail. The security of his leader would be of the utmost importance to the commander over the coming days, and Aryan would not stray far from the Emperor's side. He would remain in the shadows, his eyes on the circle of space around Cyrus, a place where no reptile would enter without Aryan's sword at its throat.

It wasn't that difficult to understand why the commander was not fond of this event, or the coming ceremonies. They were dealing with assassins after all...

~~~~~

The King sat meditating next to the looking pool in the cavern as morning light shone through the large hole in the ceiling of rock, illuminating the gardens below. The calm serenity of the grove he was seated in did nothing to appease the torrent of thoughts running like a raging river through his mind. Something was not right. He could not see what direction to take in the scenes shown to him in the water of the pool, its visions clouded and uncertain. He felt helpless to assist or guide not only his own race, but offer counsel of any kind to the rest of the realm.

The three were truly on their own at this point, and Maxxus could not see the path which they had taken, nor could he discern where they should go next, or what fate might befall them. At times, he regretted ever asking them to take up this quest.

No matter how hard he tried, his concentration was not enough for the looking pool to show him the visions he needed to see.

Ubius entered the grove quietly, not wishing to disturb the Chameleon King. He knew that Maxxus had been troubled this last day or so, and was anxious to assist by any means possible.

"Yes, my friend?" began the King, totally aware of Ubius' presence behind him. "What news do you bring me?"

"No news, Your Grace. I was passing and thought I could bring you some Lily tea?" said Ubius, trying his best to conceal concern.

Maxxus paused for a moment, as if taking the time to fully return to the present.

"Yes, that would be wonderful. Thank you, my friend." he replied.

Ubius departed silently, leaving the King to his thoughts.

Maxxus relaxed, pondering the situation. It was certainly not the most normal of issues he was confronted with. Not being able to make sense of the obscurity in the looking pool was very unsettling to him. Nothing appeared to him even during his deepest of meditations, the fate of the three remaining
~~~~~

veiled in the gloom of the unknown.

The King exhaled deeply, unsure of what to do next. It was clear to him that his ability to see what might be happening with the friends and their quest had been compromised. He felt blinded. Nothing would come to his mind, regardless of his level of calm or openness to the cosmos. He rose from his seated position beside the looking pool, pacing slightly as his thoughts began to race. There had never been a time that he could remember when his visions had been this clouded, as if blocked. Here in Andoria, he was already virtually powerless to help the companions, but not being able to see their progress, or possible dangers ahead for them was simply crippling to his mind.

Ubius appeared once again, bringing the Chameleon King a steaming stone mug. Its aromatic essence filled the grove with the sweet smell of lilies, calming Maxxus' thoughts for a moment.

"Thank you, Ubius." said the King.

Ubius bowed, waiting a moment to see if he could indulge the chameleon mystic's conversation. It was apparent to him his leader was deeply pre-occupied of late, and felt as if he might be able to further help in some way.

"I have never had this much trouble with my visions, Ubius." began Maxxus, sipping from the hot tea. "It is a very uncomfortable feeling, and I fear for our young friends on their quest."

"Perhaps the cosmos will sort itself out, and deliver an answer to you soon, my Liege." Ubius replied quietly, searching for the right words.

Maxxus considered what his friend had said for long minutes, his eyes lost, staring off into some far off place. The steam of the tea drifted up past his scaled face, eventually disappearing in the humid air of the cavern.

"I only held the sword once. And only for mere moments." Maxxus said, barely above a whisper.

Ubius only nodded, choosing to remain quiet while the King spoke.

"When the assault on Stigia failed during the last battles of the Great War, somehow the sword of Xanth was taken from the Emperor's grip. I still don't know how he did it, but Rasta of Andar held it high above the raging battle, even as we realized that we must retreat. The horned legions poured out of the city onto the battlefield, like a river with no end. Our forces were being cut apart before our eyes, and fleeing the battle was our only choice. The siege of Stigia had failed, but we knew that the sword had to be won, and had to be hidden far away from the Emperor."

Ubius remained silent, becoming lost in his leader's tale. Maxxus continued after another sip of the sweet smelling tea.

"We had secured the Gecko's Gate, passing back through the portal to the edge of the desert where all of our allies had met to battle Stigia. But we knew that the horned ones would be sent out to hunt for the remainder of our forces, and that the Emperor would not rest until he had the sword returned to him. It was powerful as a symbol, as well as a magical artifact. To the Stigian soldiers and warlords, it represented the power of the desert realm, the pinnacle of it being the Emperor himself. To the Emperor, it was a blade which could not be broken, and radiated power… We knew it needed to be kept from the Stigians, whatever the cost."

"Whatever happened to Rasta and the Gecko Guard, Your Grace?" asked Ubius, pondering the King's story.

A sudden sadness crossed Maxxus' face, and Ubius instantly regretted asking the question. The King took another drink from the mug, and continued.

"The Gecko Guard was a fierce militia made up of the male inhabitants of Andar. They were formed after the burning of the treetop city of Embrinn, the anole kingdom. A young Stigian warlord made his name well known to the rest of the realm, a Uromastyx named Cyrus Malthor. The survivors of the city fled to Andar, and the militia came forward to defend Evaria from the Emperor's thirst for conquest. The leader of this group was a tenacious young gecko named Rasta. He was a skilled hunter, and as it turned out, a brilliant tactician. It was he and his brethren in the Gecko guard who used the Gecko's Gate, an artifact forged here in Andoria by a few of us to assist in the Wars. Rasta used it to outsmart the Emperor, and his young warlord, stealing the Sword of Xanth, and escaping with it before he could be caught."

Ubius took it all in, not saying a word as the pieces of the story fell into place for him. He had read of the Great Wars in the scrolls of the archives but had not heard the tale recounted by the King, who had lived through those times. The look of awe on his scaled face was not lost on the King as he finished off his tea, and finished his story as well.

"Once the sword was in our keep, Rasta and several of the Guard headed west, travelling toward the deepest parts of the rainforest in an attempt to hide it for all time, while the remainder of our forces returned home with the Gate, to hide it as well. I never saw my friend again, although two geckos returned eventually to inform us that the task had been accomplished. The two died mysteriously within days, and our secret was safe, lost in the depths of the jungle to the west."

"You said the sword is unbreakable?" asked Ubius.

Maxxus looked up from his empty mug.

"It is not only unbreakable, but the blade is forged of a strange metal created from the desert sands. It is highly brilliant metal, capable of blinding the opponent of the reptile who wields it. It gave the Emperor a great advantage in battle, as well as being a symbol of strength and power." said the King.

"I can see why the Emperor of Stigia would desire to have the sword returned to him." replied Ubius.

"Those Emperors are long gone, my friend. The new Emperor, Cyrus, will stop at nothing to see it is returned to him, but not for the glory of Stigia. For his own glory, which is something which should be feared even more…" said Maxxus somberly.

~~~~~

The city gates were already swung wide as the Nostrian caravan approached the dark spires of Stigia, the tall stone walls bristling with horned soldiers standing respectfully at attention. Copper spear tips and shields glinted in the afternoon sun, and red capes billowed in the slight breeze of the desert.

It was obvious to Taran, Lord of Nostria, that this pageantry of Stigian military power was on display for a purpose. It was a projection of strength. The Emperor wanted to be seen as the main pillar of leadership in the realm, as though he did not need treaties or alliances with any of the other races. The Nostrian's were here because he had allowed it, not because he needed anything from them. Taran knew all too well that if Cyrus Malthor thought that Stigia needed something, they would simply step in and take it by force if it was that necessary. He watched out of one of the windows of the grand carriage as it lumbered toward the gatehouse.

The first of the caravan to enter the gates were the riders, guiding their giant iguanas through the gatehouse and onto the cobblestone of the main courtyard. The assassins followed them on foot. Finally, the great carriage, and the smaller supply carriages lumbered through, the massive beetles hauling them barely able to get through the gates.

The entire entourage managed to assemble in the courtyard, its cobblestone surface swept almost perfectly clean of the desert sands which normally filled every crack and crevice in Stigia. A small contingent of the Emperor's Royal Guard stood at attention toward the back of the courtyard, next to the entrance to the keep and its dark spires above.
~~~~~

A set of decorative wooden stairs was brought up to the side of the great carriage, and shortly after, the Lord of Nostria, his daughter, and the female attendants to the princess stepped down into the courtyard.

Despite their arrival, it was fairly quiet in the city. There were no horns to announce their arrival, there was no Emperor and his entourage to greet them. The group of monitors looked about, seeing little other than the Stigian soldiers manning the walls, and the Royal Guards. Here and there were straggling citizens of the city, observing the group curiously.

After a few moments, an older, shorter horned lizard emerged from the doors of the keep, followed by several more royal guards. He made his way toward the group of monitors, not in any kind of hurry. Taran could see by his clothing that this reptile was of some importance in Stigia, and bowed his head politely to him as he approached them.

"I am Vitos. I am glad that you have arrived, and we will see to your arrangements immediately. The Emperor regrets not being able to greet you himself, but will meet with all of you once you are settled, and his affairs are concluded..." he said.

With barely another word, except to issue instructions to a nearby soldier, Vitos motioned to several servants waiting just inside the large wooden doors of the keep. They rushed out of the shade of the entrance and began assisting the monitors who were beginning to unload the supply carriages.

Taran turned toward his daughter, whose eyes met his with confusion in them. This was no way to be greeted by her future husband. He could tell that she did not approve of this at all. He simply sighed, gave her the best smile he could muster, and turned to head toward the keep.

She waited a few moments more, feeling the heat of the desert sun, and looking up to the dark spires above. She could not see a reptile in any of the windows of the keep, even though she could sense that she was being watched. This land and this way of being treated were alien to her. She breathed in deeply, and Yokady and Maily appeared suddenly at her side. They said nothing, simply trading sympathetic glances with the princess and each other.

Finally, Yami decided to remain strong, and entered the keep, her assistants beside her. She held herself straight with her head up, ignoring the soldiers in the courtyard. She would make the best of this existence, and she would find a place of importance here amongst these desert dwellers, whether the Emperor approved of it or not. Just because it was her duty to do as her father commanded, did not mean that she could not carve out a meaningful life for herself in Stigia. She had been schooled in manners of etiquette and protocol, and knew that she could conduct herself accordingly no matter what the situation. There would surely be opportunities that would present themselves to enable her independence to some degree.

They walked through the main halls of the keep, and several servants directed them up a grand stairway to the second floor, where more attendants were waiting by the open doors of a collection of rooms. The floors were polished black stone, and the braziers and torches along the walls reflected off its dark surface. They were ushered quickly into a main room, where Taran was waiting. This room was a central sitting area, with sleeping areas off the main room through ornate doors. A single large open window looked down onto the courtyard where they had arrived, allowing a warm desert breeze in. There was already food set out on a large, low stone table around which was an assembly of comfortable looking chairs.

The Lord was seated, and several reptiles were delivering their personal items from the caravan as Yami sat down. Her assistants flocked to a room which was being appointed for the princess, keeping themselves busy.

"I know this is uncomfortable for you, my dear, but please try to remain calm and focused." said Taran.

"It is not the way things should be done, my Lord." she replied, being overly formal with her father.

He gave her a soft smile.

"If your mother were here, she would tell you how beautiful you look." he said, paying no attention to her ill temper.

She simply looked at him, and he could see the pleading look in her yellow eyes. It saddened him for a moment. She was his only hatchling, and knew little of the pain he had endured when her mother had passed from this world. She had never known her mother, other than the memories he had shared with her.

But this was a necessary move, both for Nostria, and their family. All of his efforts to create a stronger more prosperous existence for his race came down to this arrangement. Taran sighed deeply, watching his daughter's sullen face as she simply stared at the polished floor now.

The old male monitor lizard looked out the large window in the room, his eyes scanning the desert sands beyond the walls of the city. It was much cooler here in the keep, the thick stone walls shielding against the heat of the sun. Sheer draperies blew lightly in the breeze, and created an atmosphere that was cool and dry, without being stagnant. The servants placed out trinkets and carvings on the tables of the room from Nostria, and a tapestry was hung on one of the walls which depicted the training guilds of the badlands. It was intended to make them feel more comfortable, full of imagery that was familiar.

The princess simply continued to sulk. She knew that this would be her fate, her place of office from here forward.

They were interrupted from their thoughts as Vitos appeared once again in the open doorway to the suite of rooms. His polite bow was all that was offered as a result of his sudden intrusion.

"The Emperor will see all of you first thing in the morning..." he said, leaving two royal guards to guard the main entry doors to their quarters. "I suggest you rest from your long journey. Food and refreshment will be brought for all of you shortly."

He did not remain in the room a moment longer.

Yami's eyes went back to her father, as he rose from the comfort of the plush chair he was sitting in, already yawning in fatigue. He could see that look in her eyes again. It was as though she was ready to plead with him. But the horned one was right. It had been a very long trip, and it was getting late in the day. As he turned to leave the room in search of a comfortable bed, his daughter's word rang out behind him.

"This is not the way that these matters should be conducted..." she said.

12

Kiko and Alibesh had fallen asleep watching each other. Chase kept still in the undergrowth, trying to remain alert in his vigil, despite his exhaustion. Early morning light began to illuminate the rainforest canopy above, and brought a light mist along with it. The night songs of the insects had slowly begun to go silent, and birds had taken over the chorus.

Chase hoped that the horned soldiers had given up their search for the female gecko now in their midst. He still did not have the whole story about why they were after her, but it really didn't matter at this point. Her very presence had endangered all of them. The soldiers represented a real headache to him, complicating their search for the Grove. Even though there were only two of them, they might prove to be formidable opponents to them. Chase preferred to avoid them as opposed to anything else. The other side of his thoughts struggled with the idea that they might bring back more troops from Stigia if they were allowed to escape. He could only hope that they would somehow find this artifact in the Glowing Grove, and be gone long before it became an issue.

His vertically slit eyes fell on Kiko and Alibesh. They slept further apart than any of them, resting in poses that would allow them to see one another, as if they might jump up ready to fight one another at any moment. It had quickly become clear to him that they had a serious dislike and lack of trust for one another.

Kiko had been Chase's friend since they had been hatchlings. She had always enjoyed tagging along with Chase and Jonas, sharing in their adventures and mischief. Although she was an anole, she had fit in amongst every other reptile who inhabited their village like the missing piece of a puzzle. Chase watched her as she slept peacefully, with a fondness in his eyes. She had become very special to him, in ways he was not sure that he fully understood yet. Kiko had been with him for forever it seemed, as a childhood friend, and now much more. He wished that they were not here, in the middle of the rainforest, on yet another quest. The simple days were the best to him. Days where they awoke, hunted for food for the village in the warmth and peace of the familiar part of the jungle, swam in the river, and spent evenings listening to Lanwyn's stories in the Great Hall. Their lives were far more complicated once again. Chase found himself wondering for a moment what she would be like as a mother. He was certain that she would be loving, yet firm. That she would raise a hatchling to be strong and independent, whether it was a male or female. He could see the scene in his thoughts of her playing with a young one, and being a very happy mother.

He shook the thoughts from his tired mind, realizing that he was smiling to himself. He had to remain vigilant. It would soon be time for them to wake, to keep moving westward toward where he thought the Grove might be. Chase yawned, trying to move without making a sound to aid him staying awake. He was still trying to keep his sense of direction, remember the path that he had made in his mind toward their destination that he had spied from the treetops.

He now looked at the sleeping form of the female gecko, Alibesh. She rested, dressed in a tattered tunic, wrapped up in the jungle greenery. Her breathing was easy and slow, and her peaceful slumber showed no signs of restlessness or fear of being discovered by those who searched the jungle for her. Her outstretched arm supported her head, and Chase's eyes lingered on her. He could feel his face flush, as if he were hoping no one would know that he was looking at her. Something suddenly drew his eyes back to her arm. There was a blemish of some sort on the exposed underside of her wrist. No, not a blemish, a mark. He inadvertently gasped quietly in astonishment. There were four scales which were jet black, arranged in a diamond shape, which stood out against the rest of the lighter colour of her wrist. It was the mark that the Chronicler had spoken of.

"Quit staring at me..." said Alibesh quietly, her eyes still closed.

Her words startled Chase, and he quickly lowered his eyes.

"I-I'm sorry" he whispered. "I'm tired. Staring off into space is all."

He kept his face lowered as she roused from her comfortable position, attempting to hide his embarrassment at being caught watching her.

She glanced over at Kiko, who was still sleeping peacefully. Reclining in the soft mosses of the rainforest floor, Alibesh seemed in no rush to get moving. She wiped the moisture from the scales of her forehead, sensing that Chase still had many questions for her.

Chase raised his eyes again, letting his vertically slit irises trace the lines of her body as she lounged silently in the undergrowth. The first shafts of early sunlight pierced the rainforest canopy, creating knives of pure light in the slight mist.

"You're doing it again..." she whispered, keeping an eye on the sleeping form of the female anole not far away.

"I am just amazed that you are from the plains." he replied simply.

"In Sedda we refer to them as the grasslands..." she purred sarcastically, finally turning her gaze in his direction.

"You never thought about coming to Andar?" he asked.

She turned her face upward, toward the jungle canopy. Her eyes seemed to become lost as her mind went back in time.

"My parents were both killed by the horned ones, and I realized then, even as young as I was that I would never be safe counting on others to protect me." she said.

Chase considered her words for long minutes.

"I'm sorry about your parents." was all he could say, feeling dumb immediately after speaking the words.

"Why?" she replied without looking at him. "It was long ago, and you did not know me or them..."

The words stung him. She was not like any other reptile he had ever met, and the way she seemed to have no feelings about certain issues confused him. He started to formulate a reply, but decided at the last moment that it might be best to remain silent. It might be better not to risk further interest in her past if she continued to be sarcastic or even hurtful in responding.

"I'm sorry." she said, as if sensing his thoughts. "I am not used to discussing these things."

She continued to look upward, not wishing to engage in further conversation that might prove uncomfortable to either of them.

"Perhaps you should just keep your scaled lips shut, and get ready to move, or better yet, stay here while we go without you..."

The voice was Kiko's, and she opened her eyes slowly, relaxing her arms in the growth of the forest floor. Chase and Alibesh could now see the leaves and greenery move as Kiko's bowstring went slack, the arrow that had been set, carefully removed and stuck back in the quiver on her back. She had been pointing it at the female gecko the entire time.

Alibesh simply grinned as Kiko finally sat up, the two keeping their eyes locked on one another.

"Wow. It feels like the ice fields here right now." said Jonas, also sitting up out of the jungle growth.

Dantis, also finally roused himself, rustling around to find his axe, still half awake. His orbital eyes independently traced over the group.

"What's going on? How long was I asleep?" he asked, confused.

Jonas and Chase chuckled slightly, watching as the large chameleon got his bearings eventually.

The companions stood, gathering their things, and Chase scanned the forest around them, conscious once again that the two horned soldiers were still out there somewhere, searching for them.

"They are nowhere near here." said Alibesh, reading his thoughts again.

"Well, I guess there is no reason at all to worry then, except that you ended up leading them right to us, making it that much more difficult to accomplish our task..." retorted Kiko as she stepped to the edge of the clearing, ready for another day of hiking through the jungle.

"Why is it that you hate me so much, anole?" Alibesh asked her.

Kiko stopped, turning to lock eyes with the female gecko again.

"Oh, I don't hate you. But I trust you about as much as I would trust a serpent..."

<center>~~~~~</center>

The throne room was cool and dimly lit. It was early in the day, and the heat of the desert had not yet penetrated the thick stone walls of the keep. The polished onyx floors were like a mirror of black, reflecting the light coming in from a single large open window at one side of the room, which looked out over the main courtyard. The emperor was seated on his dark throne, speaking with Vitos in low tones as the Nostrians were escorted in. Cyrus' expression barely changed as his eyes raised to meet theirs.

"Welcome to Stigia. I trust that your quarters were well appointed for you and comforting so far away from your homes..." he said, almost hissing slightly.

He waved absently at Vitos, motioning him away. The old horned lizard retreated from the Emperor's side, but remained nearby. Cyrus had been discussing sending troops to find and kill the escaped female gecko and the assassin, and continue the search for the artifact that he needed. Despite his ambivalence toward the reptiles in front of him, even he knew to keep his discussion quiet. It would not have been proper for his guests from Nostria to discover that he was planning to kill one of their brethren, Amilkar. It had

~114~

been yet another aggravation to the Emperor that he had escaped the city along with the female gecko. Cyrus did not like loose ends, nor did he like the fact that Alibesh had defied him instead of accepting the great honour he had intended for her. It was an outrage that the Emperor was not about to forget easily.

Now, of course, he had to keep his attention on his guests from the northern badlands. If his plans were to reach fruition, then he would have to convince these monitors that his intentions were indeed sincere.

His eyes shifted from the aging leader of Nostria, to his daughter and her female attendants. He nodded politely to her, his eyes lingering over her beauty, without betraying any emotion. She was beautiful indeed, and Cyrus' gaze softened slightly. Taran cleared his thought slightly, and Cyrus immediately shifted his eyes to the old male monitor.

The monitor bowed graciously for the emperor, the others with him following his lead.

"Yes, thank you, Your Grace. Your hospitality is very much appreciated." said Taran.

"Your assassins have taken up quarters within the barracks in the city, and should receive good treatment by the rest of the armies. My commanders have seen to it." replied Cyrus.

Again, Taran gave a deep bow, wanting to appear grateful for all that had been provided for them. To insult the Emperor in any way at this point would never be forgotten, and would be a hindrance going forward in solidifying the relationship between their two races. The old monitor very much wanted to be the leader of their people who was responsible for ensuring not only his kingdom's survival and well-being, but its future prosperity.

His attention was diverted suddenly by his daughter fidgeting slightly beside him. He only turned his eyes her way, and she reluctantly ceased. Taran returned his gaze to the Emperor.

"My daughter is most excited for the ceremony, and wishes to convey her respects to you upon becoming your betrothed, Your Grace." he said.

He did not have to look her way to see the blood rush into her face at the thought of becoming married to the creature seated in front of her. He knew that she would ultimately do as she was asked, in the name of her homeland, even if it were not the most pleasing to her, and for a moment, the old monitor felt a pang of remorse for her. He wrestled with the thought that this was necessary for the good of his people momentarily.

The Emperor could see that there was uncertainty in the eyes of the Princess, even as she kept her gaze lowered away from him. This only served to agitate him, as he did not have time to caudle her feelings on the matter. He gripped the arm of the throne tighter, betraying his irritation.

"Perhaps the Princess and her servants would enjoy a guided tour of the city?" asked Cyrus, waving a clawed hand at them.

Yami now looked up at the Emperor, a slight look of defiance on her scaled face. She saw the perfect opportunity to assert herself during this first meeting.

"Maily, Yokady and Joa are not my servants, Your Grace…" she said, motioning toward the three other female monitors around her. "In Nostria we do not believe in having 'servants'. They have been my friends since we were very young, and they chose to come with me to assist in whatever was needed on this journey."

Taran held his breath for a moment, seeing the Emperor's eyes flare, and even the nearby guards express silent looks of shock at her words. He immediately interjected, to try to keep the situation from becoming hostile.

"I am sure that my daughter and her companions would find a grand tour very educational, while we discuss business, Your Grace." he said quickly, shooting Yami an angry glance before giving the Emperor yet another bow.

Cyrus settled back slightly on the throne, continuing to stare angrily at the female monitor. Instantly, the realization came to him that he would have to adjust her manners when speaking to him. Allowing the insolence she had just demonstrated to continue would show weakness, something he would never permit. He rose from the throne, stepping forward as all who were gathered in the room took a knee before him quickly. He waited a moment before speaking again for dramatic effect. Taran's gaze was on the floor in submission.

"Vitos, please escort the Princess and her… *friends* on a grand tour of the city. Taran and I will discuss business ahead of the ceremony." hissed the Emperor sarcastically, eyeing the group.

"Very well, Your Grace!" bowed Vitos, coming forward to usher the group from the throne room as quickly as possible.

Vitos knew full well that his leader's patience had all but run out. The balance of this situation was delicate, and the old horned lizard wanted to defuse the moment, and remove the monitors from the room immediately. It was clear that the Nostrian Princess had her own thoughts, which were a great danger to her here in Stigia. Especially when she voiced those thoughts in front of the Emperor.

"The Emperor will speak to you in your own quarters…" Vitos said quietly to Taran as he waved all of them out the large wooden doors of the throne room.

They moved out gracefully, Taran casting a quick glance back at the throne, where Cyrus still stood, motioning to one of the soldiers who had remained in the shadows at the edge of the room, silent. Even as the huge doors of the room closed with a dull boom, the Lord of Nostria had dark thoughts sweep over him, a fleeting shadow which made him feel very uneasy.

13

The companions made their way through the thick growth of the jungle, fighting and hacking at the vines and foliage to get mere feet forward.

Dantis lead the way, swinging his axe into the underbrush to clear a path for the others to follow. The humidity was thick and heavy, making each step they fought forward seem all the more exhausting.

It had been this way for most of the day, and it was as though they were moving in slow motion.

Chase moved along behind Dantis, hoping that soon the rainforest would eventually release its invisible grip on them. He wiped moisture from his scales, exhaling deeply as he watched the big chameleon fight his way through the vines and tangling greenery. They had taken turns chopping their way ahead, but Dantis was clearly the best at it.

Chase followed behind, with the others, ready to give the large reptile a break when he needed to rest. He hoped they were heading in the right direction still, without the stars to guide him, and the thick undergrowth, it was difficult for him to tell with any certainty. He had tried to push any thoughts away that they might miss the grove by accident, and run out of supplies this deep in the rainforest. It would add to their problems to have to hunt for food and drinking water while they fought to keep moving. The sudden appearance of Alibesh had already taxed their dwindling rations. And Kiko, for one was not very happy about that fact.

The gecko shook the thoughts, turning his attention back to Dantis.

"You want me to take over for a while?" he asked.

The big chameleon stopped only for a moment, breathing heavily.

"I'm OK..." he replied simply, getting a better grip on his axe before taking another hard swing into a tangle of vines.

The others followed behind him, with Alibesh bringing up the rear. They were all coated in moisture from the heavy humidity of the jungle, looking exhausted as they picked their way through the felled growth.

Chase's mind began to wander again, his thoughts on the female gecko following behind, and her tattered tunic. He could feel the blood rush to his face, imagining how she looked, without looking back. Kiko was at his back, and the gecko knew that the two shared no love for one another.

He pushed the thoughts aside as he helped Dantis pull some of the vines aside, clearing another few feet ahead of them. Were they on the right path toward the Glowing Grove? Perhaps in the blur of the last day or so they had shifted course, or walked right through it during the day, without knowing!

"We should be travelling at night..." said Alibesh, echoing Chase's thoughts.

Kiko stopped. She turned toward the female gecko with a snarl on her face.

"Yes, well, it would be REAL easy to hack our way through this in the dark!" she said sarcastically, motioning toward the thick growth all around them.

"The forest has to get easier to travel through eventually!" Alibesh shot back quickly.

"Spoken like a lizard who has never lived in the rainforest!" Kiko continued.

Chase moved in between the two of them as they stepped toward one another, certain that their argument might become physical at any moment. Dantis stopped his assault on the growth with his axe to see what was going on, and Jonas simply grinned slightly at the two females bickering.

"Can we all just be calm for a moment?" Chase asked quietly, looking to each of them.

They refrained from any other angry words, relaxing slightly. There was a few moments of silence between the group of reptiles, and they just rested for a bit, listening as the birds and insects resumed their songs in the absence of the shouting or the chopping of undergrowth.

Dantis finally dropped his axe, sitting down heavily in a heap of exhaustion amongst the cut up vines. Looking back to the two females, Chase exhaled deeply, frustration in his voice as he spoke.

"I wish you two could just quit with the stand-off for a while..." he said.

Alibesh showed no change in her expression, but Kiko shot the male gecko an injured look. Chase ignored it as best he could, turning toward the wall of thick growth that Dantis had been working to cut through. He drew his sword, the silver steel letting out a light screech as it came out of its scabbard. The gecko gripped it tightly, stepping past his big chameleon friend. Without another word, he took over the work, cutting savagely at the jungle ahead. As if possessed, Chase erased the concerns of their quest, forgot the two arguing females, and just focused on moving forward.

As another few hours passed, he felt as if he was moving ever quicker through the greenery which held all of them hostage. It was not an illusion, it was a simple matter of the jungle becoming more open gradually, with less of the thick growth holding him back. The way became slowly easier, until he only occasionally had to cut a few vines to walk ahead.

They emerged into a large clearing, and Chase stopped suddenly, seeing something ahead which did not fit. The afternoon had now faded to dusk, and the shadows had once again grown deeper. The strange thing that he was seeing did not make sense to him. The others stopped as well, sensing Chase's caution immediately. Kiko let a slight gasp escape her.

On the forest floor in this clearing, shrouded in the green leaves and mosses of the rainforest, was the bleached white skeleton of a reptile, lying prone on its back. A bright flash of the dying light caught the gecko's eyes. There was something silver sticking out of the skeletal remains. Chase stepped slowly closer, his sword still at the ready.

The skeleton had been there for a long time. The jungle's vines and low growth had grown into it, as if to protect the fallen reptile's remains. The leaves cradled it, as if this creature might someday rise again. Moss covered tatters of a cape, and rusted armour lay nearby, but Chase kept his attention focused on the silver object between two of the skeletal ribs. It was a dagger, its hilt encrusted with three gemstones on each side.

There were no markings on the armour, nothing to tell this skeleton's story. Chase could not tell for sure, but he thought it might even be the bones of a gecko. It was definitely not a chameleon, missing the high casque on its head, and most likely not an anole, for it would be much slimmer. He knew it was not an amphibian either, which ruled out the races of frogs and toads.

The friends gathered around it, and Chase gently removed the dagger from between its ribs. Dantis looked at it in wonder.

"That was definitely made in Andoria..." he said softly, both his orbital eyes trained on the silver blade.

The male gecko rolled it over, inspecting it from all sides. It was beautiful. But what was it, and this skeletal reptile, doing out here this deep in the rainforest?

Jonas practically dropped beside Chase, and for the first time, the gecko realized that they were all very tired. The light was fading.

"Let's make camp for the night." said Chase, tucking the dagger into his sword belt.

"Here? This seems like it might be a bad spot, don't you think?" asked Jonas, pointing at the skeletal remains. "It doesn't seem like this guy had much luck here!"

"It's fine." replied Chase simply.

The others began to lay out blankets, thankful that they would be able to rest finally, now that they had fought their way through the toughest bush any of them had had to traverse in their lives. They ate and drank a little, ready to sleep now that the forest was becoming cool and dark. Night sounds began to come alive around them, and a sense of peace fell upon them.

All of them but Chase. He ate and drank very little, and instead began to rummage around the clearing for just the right piece of bark from one of the many massive tree trunks. The others watched him, looking on strangely as he began to dig into the soft mosses, exposing the rich earth, and digging down into that as well. He made a deep hole eventually in a corner of the clearing, and the others finally realized what he was up to. He was digging a grave.

Even if they thought it was odd, not one of them uttered a word. For whatever reason, Chase felt compelled to do it, to bury the skeletal remains as if he could bring its soul peace at last.

When he finally finished, he stuck a piece of wood in the earth, carved with a crude message to identify its place, and the unknown soul that it represented. He sat for a moment in the dark, the remnants of a small fire the others had made burning behind him. His scaled were covered in dirt, and he laid on his side, totally exhausted. Sleep took him quickly, but he grinned slightly as he entered his slumber, feeling that somehow, for some unknown reason, he had done the right thing.

~~~~~

The commander listened intently as the Emperor spoke to him in low tones. His face betrayed no emotion as he received his instructions from the Stigian leader, his steely eyes fixed and thoughtful, his posture rigidly at attention as his position in the plot was revealed to him.

"Send your troops to the southern regions of the deep rainforest, where our maps show the thickest undergrowth. It is there that you will find this Glowing Grove, and recover the sword." he said, his eyes locked with Aryan's.

"It will take two days to cross the Sand Sea, so I will send a forward unit using our wasps, they can be there much quicker." replied the commander
~~~~~

quietly.

Cyrus considered his words for a moment.

"An excellent idea, Commander." he began. "There will be great reward for you in the future if you succeed in this. If your soldiers happen to encounter that female gecko or the assassin in their travels, kill them. I want to be finally rid of their filth."

Aryan's expression remained stoic as he digested the Emperor's words. His thoughts raced as his brain analyzed every detail of his leader's plans. They seemed almost two-dimensional thinking to Aryan, and his mind was used to looking at things in a very different way. He added things to what Cyrus described, forming a truly unique portrait of what the Emperor wanted to accomplish.

"There is the possibility that we could by-pass the Grove without even realizing it, Your Grace. Or that The Three have already recovered the sword, which would drastically change the way we would need to act…" said Aryan.

The Emperor considered his Captain's ideas. Although he liked to have total control of his kingdom and preferred to keep like-minded individuals in higher positions, He had come to trust Aryan's abilities to see holes in a perspective plan. Cyrus stroked his scaled chin, thinking. He had underestimated these things in the past, and regretted it. The three had ruined his plans for years, and it would be folly to allow them to slip away again, this time with the Sword of Power in their grasp. He could not allow that to happen. To do so would be to appear weak, or stupid. And he was neither. It could even shift the balance of power in the realm this time if he were not cautious. Strategy would be of the utmost importance here.

"Perhaps it would be prudent to make the ceremony here the top priority for you, Your Grace, and worry about the sword later…" said Aryan.

Cyrus flashed him an angry look, abandoning his line of thought.

"That sword is the key to ruling all of Evaria! I will have it at all costs, Captain!" the Emperor hissed. "I plan to dispense of both the Princess and the Lord of Nostria, and send the armies north to claim the badlands as a territory of the Empire!"

"And what of the units of assassins that have accompanied the Lord and his daughter here? They will not take kindly to the killing of their leader…" asked the Captain, his face unchanged.

The Emperor straightened to his full height, glancing around to ensure no other lizard had been within earshot of their quiet conversation.

"My Royal Guardsmen will handle any of our guests who do not see the wisdom of joining Stigia. You will accompany the troops south to ensure the retrieval of the sword, Captain. That is your objective. With the Sword of Power in my grasp, and new re-enforcements from Nostria, no part of the realm will be safe from our forces."

Aryan bowed quickly without another word, turning on his heel to depart. No further talking was required, and the Captain knew he had pressed his leader far enough. As he stalked away out the doors of the throne room, a slight grin traced his lips. The lizard liked to know every part of a plan before he engaged it, and the Emperor had just divulged all of it. Cyrus' dealings with the Nostrians seemed underhanded at best, and Aryan was glad that he would be gone during that part of things. Even to him, it was a very cold thing to do. Their guests had been invited under a flag of truce, to seal a pact between the two races, and the Emperor had planned nothing more than executing the leaders, and assuming control by force. It had no honour.

The Captain continued down the halls of the keep, his red cape brushing the polished floors as he hurried to begin assembling his soldiers for the task ahead. Aryan shed his thoughts of the Nostrians, and of the Emperor, and concentrated on organizing the task ahead in his mind. His time would obviously be better spent planning his mission to recover the sword, than worry about the Emperor and his deeds.

As he emerged from the keep into the courtyard, the late day sun hit his face, and Aryan was happy to feel its radiant heat. The chill of the darkened hallways of the keep disappeared, and the Captain turned his gaze toward the stables where the wasps were all kept. His mission would not be an easy one, in a place which was mostly alien to him. He turned toward the stables, his pace quickening. Fighting in the jungle would be much different than in the open desert, he knew. But as always, he would accomplish his appointed task to perfection. He would simply take a larger force than he had initially planned…

14

Chase was certain he was dreaming. He felt warm, and could sense light before his eyes. He breathed easily, as if moving around in the space surrounding him effortlessly.

He heard something. The sounds of the insects singing their night song. Then there was another sound. A gasp. And then another. Movement. He was being moved, shaken. Shaken.

"Chase... Wake up. You have to see this!" a voice spoke to him.

"Chase!" again the voice spoke, more urgent this time. It was Kiko.

He opened his eyes. What met his sight was something he did not understand. There was light everywhere, despite the fact that his body told him it was the middle of the night. A fern draped over him, its leaves brilliant with some kind of green light within itself. A vine hung next to it, a deep purple hue emanating from it, all the way along its stem up into the canopy, its leaves bold and full of a purple glow.

Chase turned his head, only to see the soft green and blue glow from the mosses that he laid upon. Mushrooms sprang from the forest floor like lamps, bathing the ground in their blue light, and various clumps of tropical growth punctuated the forest in hues of red and yellow radiance.

There was no darkness here, and each piece of the rainforest's growth was a representative of its species, trying to outshine the others, bursting with glowing light in the night. The sounds of insects and creatures of the dark were deafening here, as if the entire forest was putting on its best display.

He sat up, taking it all in. It filled the senses, the night sounds, the thick humidity, and it was as if it were daytime. Glowing wildflowers spilled the perfume of their aromas into the night air.

The others were just as in awe of their sudden new surroundings as he was. They sat wide-eyed at the entire spectacle, lost for words in its colossal beauty. It was the most amazing sight they had ever seen.

"Now I know why they named this place what they did!" said Jonas, staring around them in disbelief.

"It's beautiful…"said Kiko.

Chase stood up, stepping over to a nearby fern. Its fronds were bright glowing green, casting its light over the mosses around it. A family of ladybugs went through the small clearing where the friends were, hurrying off in single file amongst the foliage.

As if in some sort of dream, the friends began to walk, looking in wonder at each new piece of fauna as they explored.

"If we had kept going during the day, we would have missed this entirely, without even knowing it!" said Alibesh.

"Yes, once again we have had a bit of luck." replied Chase. "Now we just have to figure out how to find the sword."

"What sword?" asked Alibesh.

Chase began to recount their quest to the female gecko as the friends walked, describing the Sword of Xanth as best he could from what Maxxus and the Chronicler had told them. He told her about the legends of the sword, how it had been forged by the first Emperor of Stigia, about it being taken away during the Great War, and hidden away to prevent Stigia from conquering all of Evaria.

Kiko suddenly cleared her throat loudly, and Chase looked her way. The female anole was giving him a look which told him that he may not want to tell this stranger everything. It was not lost on Alibesh, as she caught the look as well. She said nothing, instead changing the subject.

"So where will you all go from here?" she asked.

"We will return to Andoria first, and bring the sword to the Chameleon King. Then, with it safe, we will venture home to Andar. Hopefully, that will be the end of these quests…" Chase replied.

They fell quiet again as they continued along through the radiant growth. Narrow paths seemed to divide the Grove, as though it had been created by some force that desired to showcase the plants which gave off light in a kaleidoscope of colour.

"You all seem to care a great deal for what happens in the realm, it is very commendable." said Alibesh.

"We don't ever want to be under the rule of the tyranny of the Stigian Empire…" said Dantis.

This seemed to satisfy the female gecko, and the friends continued to stroll through the grove without further conversation. They stopped occasionally to admire the towering growth, its glow bright enough to illuminate the canopy high above. Everywhere they looked, the night was alive with colour, smells and sounds.

Chase stopped suddenly, his eyes locked on a feature ahead in the forest. It was an outcropping of rock, rising off the jungle floor, a natural high area in the midst of the Grove.

"This might be a good place to start looking…" he said.

~~~~~

Dozens of wasps landed in a large clearing inside the rainforest, as the sun sank low. The last rays of the setting sun could be seen through the canopy above as the formation touched down one by one. Their riders dismounted quickly, regrouping into one unit as more of the airborne insects landed around them. Eventually, there was a large gathering of soldiers, armed with copper swords and shields, at attention and ready to travel on foot through the thick greenery.

One soldier stood out from the rest, wearing a purple scarf over top of his red cape and copper armour. He was obviously the reptile in charge of the group, and stepped quickly forward to address the troops who still jockeyed into their ranks.

"This is as far as we can go by air, the forest becomes too thick from here, so we must go forward by land." he shouted. "Remain close together, and be watchful for this grove that glows!"

He stalked off through the rainforest undergrowth without another word, and the soldiers fell in quickly to follow him, as the contingent fought their way through the ever-thickening jungle ahead.

The sergeant who led them knew only what he had been told about where they were going, had only his orders from the captain to guide him on his mission. Find the glowing Grove, and retrieve the Sword of Power. If he found the three, or the escaped prisoners from Stigia, kill them.

But the environment was as much their enemy as the three reptiles of the prophecy. It fought against their advance into the depths of the forest, as if it would hold them back from discovering its secrets. The Stigian soldiers slashed at vines and branches, carving their way forward.

The sergeant would not rest, nor would he let his troops, until they accomplished their mission. This task had been handed down from the Emperor himself, and this reptile and his soldiers had no desire to fail their leader.
~~~~~

Some of the soldiers had been equipped to carry extra food and water, and they continually provided the troops that were cutting through the forest fresh water and food to retain their strength while others rested. In this manner, the Stigians cut a path through the rainforest much more quickly. The heat and humidity was stifling to these lizards, much more used to the arid heat of the desert as they were. None of this however, slowed the advance of the column through the tangling jungle growth.

The sergeant stopped for a drink of fresh cool water from his water skin, assessing the rough map he had been given by his Captain. It was nearly night now, and his troops had cut their way through a great deal of the forest. He scanned the surrounding growth, hoping for any sign of the place they were looking for. He had been briefed on where the Grove was believed to be, but it was very different out in the field. It was even difficult to ascertain whether they were heading in a straight line across the jungle, as they had passed through hills and valleys that could not be seen from above the canopy overhead.

There was the hum of insect wings again, and the sergeant glanced back behind, to see three more wasps landing in the path they had cut. It was the Captain, and two other lieutenants escorting him.

Aryan dismounted, making his way through the growth toward the sergeant. It was getting late in the day, but the soldiers quickened their pace as best they could at the sight of their Captain.

"I see that good progress is being made..." Aryan said to the sergeant as he approached, surveying the path that had been made through the thick rainforest growth.

"Yes sir. We have been cutting forward very well." replied the lizard promptly.

The Captain watched the horned soldiers work at the growth, moving forward as they chopped and slashed at the undergrowth. Others rested, switching off with the lizards at the front as they became tired.

Darkness began to fall in the jungle around them, and the sounds of night began to sound out from the thick undergrowth.

"Your orders, Sir?" asked the sergeant.

Aryan continued to watch the soldiers cutting their way through the forest.

"Light enough torches so that the troops can keep working." he replied with no emotion in his voice.

"When shall we allow them to rest?" pressed the sergeant.

The Captain looked directly at him now, and all that could be seen in his eyes was icy resolve.

"Do you have this Sword that the Emperor desires?" he asked.

"No Sir." came the quick response.

"Then they shall rest when we find the Glowing Grove. They will rest when we have the Sword of Power..."

~~~~~

Chase and Alibesh looked down onto the pools of bronze liquid bubbling in the rock, momentarily mesmerized by its shimmering colour. Glowing ferns draped around them, their soft green light illuminating the surface of the outcropping. Heat radiated off the liquid metal.

Alibesh knelt cautiously, her vertically slit eyes scanning the pools for any sign of their quarry. If the sword was indeed here, then how would they retrieve it? Her thoughts swirled as the liquid metal boiled and bubbled, a slight metallic smell filling her senses.

Chase too watched carefully, searching the pools for anything that might tell them that the sword was hidden here.

The others looked around the grove, still in a state of shock at the beauty of their luminescent surroundings. Kiko and Jonas had discovered a clump of wild berries, each one giving off bright red light. Jonas was already licking his lips at the thought of fresh wild food.

"I don't think that would be a good idea, we really don't know anything about them. They could be poisonous!" she said.

"Oh, come on!" Jonas complained. "Just one won't hurt me!"

He reached out to pick one of the tiny glowing fruits, just as Dantis appeared to see what they were doing.

"Let him eat it," Dantis chuckled quietly to Kiko. "Maybe it will make him glow! We can use him for a torch later!"

Jonas took a playful swipe at the big chameleon. Once again he reached into the glowing shrub, pulling one of the berries from its stem. Immediately, its glow extinguished, as if it had been disconnected from some kind of magical energy source.

"There, you see? You just wrecked it!" Kiko exclaimed with a grin.

Jonas frowned at the statement, not sure about what to do now. He simply placed the berry into his pack, to make a decision on its fate later.

"Just like a hatchling, gotta mess with everything..." said Dantis sarcastically.
~~~~~

Back on the rock outcropping, Chase and Alibesh had resorted to a new tactic to explore the pools of liquid bronze. They had found sticks to probe the depths of the ponding metal. This did not work well, as the sticks melted almost immediately. It was apparent that they would find nothing in this manner. Chase removed a piece of his silver leg armour, dipping a small edge of it into one of the pools. It too melted rather quickly, and he removed it immediately to cool before strapping it back on. He shrugged to the female gecko, unsure of what to do next.

"This is going to be more difficult than I thought..." remarked Chase.

"There must be some way to do this!" said Alibesh in frustration.

She sighed deeply, plopping herself down on the rock, her eyes again focusing on the bubbling bronze. Kiko, Jonas, and Dantis now appeared, and looked in awe at the scene in front of them.

"Don't touch anything..." Dantis said to Jonas, chuckling again and giving the gecko a nudge.

Jonas only returned an indignant gaze to the chameleon.

"So how do we know what is in there?" Asked Kiko, kneeling by one of the pools.

She could feel the heat from it, and sat back quickly as a large bubble erupted, threatening to splash liquid metal at her.

"Well, we have tried several things, and now we are looking for any new ideas?" Chase replied, looking around at them curiously.

They each seemed to be lost in thought, watching the bubbling liquid.

"Maybe we could just dip Jonas in there!" joked Dantis again, playfully.

Jonas pretended to ignore him, instead trying to come up with something that his friends had not tried yet. He withdrew his sword, but Chase and Alibesh both shook their heads at him, Chase showing his friend the melted edge of his leg armour. He focused again, much to the amused looks of Kiko and Dantis.

"Try not to hurt yourself, thinking so hard!" said Kiko.

This was the last straw for Jonas. Tired of being the butt of their jokes, he raised his arms in exasperation, giving them a foul look.

"Why aren't you two taking any of this seriously?!" he asked.

Kiko and Dantis simply laughed at the gecko in reply, and even Chase caught himself smiling. Jonas sheathed his silver blade, putting his hands on his hips and looking around at them with a grimace of impatience. He stalked over toward the edge of one of the pools of bronze for a closer look, determined to find a way to see what might be in their depths. He tripped on a ripple in the rock, falling forward too quickly to catch himself. Before the others could react, Jonas tumbled into Alibesh, spilling the two of them forward on the rock. Alibesh was very near the side of one of the pools. Too close. She fell forward, only able to break her fall with one scaled hand. The other went into the liquid metal, its bubbling surface splashed by the impact of her hand and wrist into it.

The others gasped, and Chase reached forward instantly, pulling the female gecko backward, even though he knew the damage had been done. She would be lucky to have a hand left at all, his mind registered. He and Alibesh collapsed in a heap on the outcropping, and the others scrambled quickly to help the two reptiles up from where they lie on the rock.

Alibesh shook herself off a bit, her hand tucked into the folds of her tunic. The friends could only imagine the burned flesh that remained after being fully immersed in the bronze liquid of the pools. But there was no pain on the female gecko's face. It was a look of surprise. As she pulled her hand out to look at it, the others could see why.

There was not a blemish on her scales, her hand perfectly intact, as if the entire event had never happened. Alibesh rolled her hand back and forth, a look of utter astonishment in her eyes, which was mirrored by the rest of the group.

"Are you OK?" was all that would fall from Jonas' lips, as he stared at her apologetically.

"Yes, I think I am quite alright..." said Alibesh, still looking at her hand.

Chase remembered what the old toad had told them, about the 'one who bore the mark'. It was the diamond mark on Alibesh's scales! She was the one who could find the sword! His eyes were fixed on the cluster of black scales on the underside of Alibesh's wrist as he now fully realized that they could finally accomplish their quest!

"Alibesh is the one the Chronicler spoke of! She can retrieve the sword from the pools. Look at the mark on her wrist..." Chase said aloud, pointing to the female gecko.

Alibesh drew her hand back instinctively, as if she were worried of being bitten by some unseen creature. She looked around at the others suspiciously.

"Who is the Chronicler?" she asked. "And what mark are you speaking of?"

Chase stumbled through the story quickly, ignoring Alibesh's looks about obvious disbelief, describing their quest for the Sword of Xanth, what they had learned from the old toad, and the legends about the Glowing Grove. When he finally finished speaking, Alibesh was simply staring at him.

"So this is supposed to happen to me?" she asked, dumbfounded.

"Yes." was all Chase could reply.

The others nodded in agreement to her.

The female gecko was silent for minutes, as she strolled back toward the pool of liquid metal her hand had been submerged in. Her eyes lingered on the bubbling bronze as she knelt down beside it, seemingly mesmerized by its shimmering metallic surface. Without a word, she reached down toward the pool. The others held their breath, seeing what she was about to do. Her hand went into the liquid, and she reached in further, a tranquil look on her face. She leaned forward, her whole arm now immersed, as she felt around. Suddenly, Alibesh stopped.

Chase's eyes widened, as he could barely contain himself for what she might have found.

"Well? Did you find something?" he asked excitedly.

The others gathered in closer, and the female gecko turned toward them, a large grin filling her scaled face.

"Is this what you have been looking for?" she chimed, leaning back.

As she withdrew her arm from the bronze, the hilt of a large sword emerged, followed by the blade. It was like nothing they had ever seen before. The entire length of its wide blade was black metal, as if it had been forged from darkness itself. The guard and hilt were black as well, but blood red fabric was wrapped on the hilt. It was both beautiful and terrifying at the same time. As Alibesh lifted it from the pool, she needed to use both arms to heft it, placing both clawed hands on its long hilt.

"The Sword of Xanth!" exclaimed Chase.

The female lizard looked directly at Chase, swinging the huge sword in the air with an ease that came from many years of training.

"The Sword of Power..." corrected Alibesh.

15

Cyrus strode down the hallway of the keep, the polished floors bathed in torch light. He could sense that his carefully laid plan was coming slowly but surely to fruition. It would not be long before he had control over all of the northern badlands, folding Nostria into the Empire, its assassins bowing to him as their new leader. Taran and his daughter had no idea what the Emperor of Stigia had in store for them, and all he needed was to be wed to the Princess in order for everything to be in place.

The uromastyx smiled evilly to himself as he approached the wing of rooms that had been set up for the Nostrian guests. Two of his royal guards were positioned outside the main doors in the hallway. The guards were there to 'protect' their guests, but little did the Lord of Nostria know, they could not protect his entourage from the real danger that they faced.

Vitos approached to join his master in the hallway as Cyrus reached the doors of the wing of rooms. The Emperor turned his attention to the short, older horned lizard.

"Where is the Princess?" he asked.

"The Princess of Nostria and her companions are in the steam baths, Your Eminence. They are being pampered by the servants as we speak." Vitos replied.

He produced several rolled parchments for his leader, and Cyrus took them quickly, knowing that they were the details of the agreement between the ruler of the northern badlands and Stigia. It was a contract. But a contract as hollow and dark as the Emperor's soul, offering only words, which would be ignored the moment that Cyrus had an Empress.

The Emperor considered the words, turning to the guards with a nod. The lizards standing guard opened the thick wooden doors, stepping back quickly for their leader to enter. Cyrus motioned for Vitos to follow as he stepped into the room, his eyes quickly darting around to ensure that none of the assassins were lurking within sight. It suddenly occurred to him that this was a tactical error, one that could have cost him his life if the Lord of

Nostria had come bearing ill intentions. His Captain would have insisted that the Emperor have his guards with him at all times had he have been present.

All that Cyrus saw, however, was the old monitor, seated comfortably on the luxurious sofa, a long, low table between him and the doorway where the Emperor and Vitos had entered. He gave a simple bow of his head in respect for the two visitors, and then rose slowly, waiting for the Stigian leader to be seated in a nearby chair if he so chose.

It was obvious to Cyrus that Taran was offering up the best of Nostrian etiquette. He returned his attention to the leader of Nostria, nodding out of respect as he went to a nearby chair next to where the monitor had been sitting. He sat, motioning to Taran to once again be seated, so that they might finalize the arrangements between their two races.

The dry, cool night breeze flowed into the room from the large windows in the suite, causing the torches to flicker lightly as Cyrus laid the parchments out on the table in front of the Lord of Nostria.

"These are the details of our arrangement, which require your insignia." said the Emperor.

Taran inspected each sheet of parchment, the old monitor's eyes squinting to read the script. He had expected their agreement to be done in writing, to solidify the relationship between Stigia and Nostria. It was a logical step. But Taran wanted to do his due diligence, and ensure that there were no surprises hidden in the writing in front of him.

Cyrus sat patiently, his eyes not betraying the obvious secret that he was keeping from the leader of the northern badlands. The papers really meant nothing, and the Emperor knew it. Aryan knew it. And so did Vitos. The truth was that Nostria would not only receive nothing in the arrangements, but they were being duped into being swallowed up by the Empire. As soon as Taran put his mark on the papers, and Cyrus was wed to his daughter, his life would be worth nothing. The Emperor quietly gave Vitos a sideways glance as they waited for the Lord of Nostria to inspect the pact between them.

Taran finally put the parchments back on the table, withdrawing a quill and vial of ink from his robes. The monitor carefully began to write his insignia at the bottom of each sheet. As the ink dried, the Emperor could no longer conceal the grin on his scaled, scarred face.

"I think this arrangement will benefit both our worlds." said Taran, sitting back comfortably as Vitos collected the parchments.

Cyrus leaned forward in his chair, his eyes fixed on the monitor.

"Yes, I believe it will. You have no idea how well this will work out." he said.

~~~~~

As the friends marvelled at the sword, a sound slowly arose in the Grove. It began low and steady, barely audible at first.

Chase turned his senses to the forest around him. The sounds of the night in the rainforest had suddenly gone silent, replaced by something new. The sound was faint, but it was definite. It was a low drumming sound, as if hundreds of sticks were striking the soft ground of the jungle in succession. He craned his neck around, looking beyond the rock outcropping, as he scanned the glowing fauna. Uneasiness came to him as he could feel the ground shake slightly, the noise growing thunderous.

The friends all took a step backward, stepping off the outcropping as the sound intensified and the undergrowth began to move. Alibesh tucked the sword behind her protectively, as the others drew their weapons.

Kiko already had an arrow notched in her bow, using Dantis as cover, the big chameleon watchful, with both hands on his battle axe.

The glowing vines and vegetation shivered as the ground shook again, the drumming sound almost deafening. A shower of leaves fell from the canopy itself, shaken free from the trees that hosted them high above the Grove.

The plants of the jungle were ripped apart like a curtain as fiery eyes lit up the space between them, and long, deadly looking spiked mandibles emerged along with them. A huge long insect with hundreds of spiny legs reared up out of the forest growth, its segmented red body slick with the humidity and dew of the rainforest. Two thick clawed arms stood out just below the creature's head. It was a giant centipede.

The companions were open-mouthed at the horror before them, frozen in place by terror. It did not last long, especially for one of the friends in particular.

"OK, TIME TO RUN!!!" yelled Jonas.

The words had barely left his mouth and he was already sprinting off across the Grove, wasting no time in his escape.

The others shook off the momentary lapse, turning away from the horrific vision filling their senses in a flat out run. Kiko forgot any notion that an arrow would harm the giant insect, shouldering her bow and running through the glowing growth as fast as her legs would carry her. The others were close
~~~~~

behind, and Alibesh carried the dark blade of the Sword defensively, pointing it backward as she raced through the Grove.

The massive creature let out a strange screaming noise, the sound sharp and piercing. It crashed through the jungle growth after the reptile intruders, its mandibles clicking together hungrily. Vines and small trees snapped like twigs as the huge insect barrelled through the Grove in pursuit, the drumming of its many legs deafening in the friends' ears as they ran. It was like a wave of destruction following them, as they dodged through the rainforest, trying desperately to keep ahead of the monstrosity.

The forest ahead of them became dark, as they left the glowing foliage behind, passing the clearing, and entering the path they had cut through the thick growth. It made it easier for them to run, falling into single file in the narrow trail through the jungle, but it also made it easier for the centipede, which followed them closely. There was no place to go but forward, and they ran as fast as they could, their lungs on fire. If they tried to divert into the thick growth on either side of them, they risked becoming entangled. Even a second would be enough for the creature to be on them. The jungle whipped past as they ran, the five reptiles trying desperately to escape from the nightmare which followed close behind.

"I don't remember the toad saying anything about this!!" yelled Dantis, his breath coming in gasps.

"JUST KEEP MOVING!" shouted Chase.

It had seemed like long minutes that the chase went on, and the companions forced themselves to keep running, as the creature screamed again behind them, the hungry mandibles searching for the meal it knew was close by.

They came to the top of a rise in the forest floor, where the landscape dropped abruptly away. In the darkness, it was steeper than it appeared, and the friends began to lose their footing as they travelled downward. One by one they fell, tucking and rolling, unable to stop themselves.

In the dizzying tumble that continued, a light was discernible ahead. Although they could only hope that they would not be badly injured, they began to roll past... torches. The creature screamed once more, and Chase began to hear cries of surprise, suddenly recognizing the reptiles they were passing. They were horned soldiers!

Kiko and Jonas were the first to regain their footing as they came to the bottom of the hill, not stopping to look at the confused reptiles that had parted to the sides of the trail to avoid them as they careened down amongst them. Chase finally got his feet beneath him, reaching out for Alibesh to assist her getting up as well. She rose quickly, pulling away from him and sprinting onward. Dantis was close behind.

One lizard amongst the group could see who these tumbling reptiles were. The Captain.

"Stop them!!" Aryan commanded loudly over the commotion.

But the small group was already beyond them, and at a run again. Several of the Stigian troops drew their weapons, ready to charge off into the jungle after the companions. They stopped as the drumming sound descended upon them.

The horror came into the midst of the soldiers, grabbing anything nearby, and devouring it with its searching mandibles, its clawed arms knocking others in the gloom of the rainforest growth.

Aryan drew his sword, standing his ground. At the sight of this, several other soldiers gathered in front of the Captain, raising shields to protect him. Aryan motioned to his archers, who quickly lined up their shot against the attacker.

The creature continued its flailing frenzy, even as the Stigian troops began to fight back, slashing blindly at the massive insect. Volleys of arrows found their mark, and the centipede writhed in pain and let out piercing screams. As the soldiers finally subdued and killed it, Aryan refused to relax. He took the lieutenant and several others, heading after the reptiles who had come through their ranks. Quickly, they ran back through the dew-laden growth, searching for the escaped group. It would prove fruitless, and the Captain grabbed a torch from the soldier next to him, holding it high as they reached their transportation.

The group of wasps that had brought them into the rainforest was here, short by five, and with an unconscious guard lying in the mosses of the forest floor...

Aryan gritted his teeth in frustration. As quickly as that, the three had escaped him. Whether or not they had the Sword he had not seen, but he was inclined to believe that they did. There were two others with them, but it was of no matter. He had failed.

The Emperor would not take this incident lightly. His inability to act quickly enough had likely cost him retrieving the Sword of Power. And without it, his master would not be very happy. His instructions had been simple, and now he would have to pay the consequence. He slowly sheathed his sword, even though he wanted to rend those around him from limb to limb. It would do no good. He knew he must accept the failure as his own.

"Call the survivors back, we will head back to Stigia to re-group..." he hissed at the lieutenant.

The officer offered a quizzical look at the Captain's words.

"But Sir, should we not press forward to find the Glowing Grove? Perhaps all is not lost."

Aryan considered drawing his sword again and ending the soldier's life for his obvious stupidity. He glanced up at the canopy above, where the first traces of dawn could be seen through the leaves. The cool, grey light of day emerged, and he knew that this day might be his last.

"There is nothing left to find." he replied.

16

The Princess fidgeted with her gown relentlessly, a fact that made her companions job of readying her for the ceremony all the more difficult. Yami did not like the way that things were progressing, and she really did not have a good feeling about the Emperor himself. Her unease made it difficult for Maily, Yokady and Joa to help her with dressing, but they remained quiet nonetheless. It would be a long day, filled with small details to attend to, and they remained patient with the Princess as best they could.

Yami knew that it was important to carry out her father's wishes. Important to him, and the future of Nostria. She had a duty to her race and to her homeland. Even though she would not have chosen this for herself, she knew that she had to put her selfish thoughts aside in the end.

"It is a beautiful gown." said Yokady calmly.

The princess offered half of a smile in return, trying to distract her thoughts from the upcoming event which would change her life forever. She decided that she must focus on the positive.

Her gown was indeed beautiful, made from the finest white silks, and decorated with earth-toned polished beads from the badlands that were her home. She held a bouquet of desert wildflowers, and around the room, the Stigian servants were preparing centerpieces made of the same.

Yami's dark scales had been moisturized, shining and polished in the light of the morning sun streaming through a large window in the room. She wore a wreath of the same wildflowers around her head, along with a silk scarf which would also hide her face until the end of the ceremony.

"This will be quite a different way of life than we are used to, my friends." she said to the other female monitors toiling away at her appearance.

"We would not want to be apart from you, your highness." said Maily.

Yami looked at the young monitor fondly.

"You know you don't have to call me that, Maily." she responded.

"We are just making sure we follow the protocols for the benefit of the

Stigians, highness." said Joa with a slight giggle.

At least she had her friends with her in this place, she thought to herself, examining her look in a nearby mirror. Without them, she would have been an utter wreck. It was comforting to have them close to her. And it would be a nerve-wracking day ahead. There would be many reptiles attending this grand event, and she was worried about every little thing. The old horned lizard Vitos had run them through a brief rehearsal of the order of things when she would be brought to the throne room for the wedding, and she could only hope that she would remember everything and not embarrass herself or her father.

Doubts began to creep back into her mind about her place here in the desert kingdom, whether she would have any real duties, or whether she would be little more than a token of alliance with her homeland to the north. She was determined that she would bring about change for the citizens of Stigia, to make their simple lives more prosperous, and loosen the restrictions on their freedoms. It would be a difficult task to accomplish without angering the Emperor, who would also be her new husband. She almost shuddered at the thought. He did not exactly fit with her idea of a partner for life. Nor did she like his abrasive personality. Her smile faded as she thought of the way she might be treated by such a brutish reptile once the pleasantries of the wedding faded into the past.

"Stigia will be all the more beautiful with you here, my lady." said Yokady, putting another few flowers into the wreath on the Princess' head.

Yami simply drew a deep breath, exhaling heavily as her thoughts swirled.

"Stigia is nothing like home..." she replied.

Yokady sighed sympathetically, but did not say anymore, continuing with her task. All of their lives would change now, and to be in Nostria again would only be for a visit, if it was permitted at all. They would be expected to conform to a Stigian way of life, to accept traditions that were foreign to them, and to give up the ones that they had held their entire lives.

The Princess turned, looking out the window to the endless dunes of the Sand Sea beyond the walls of the city, feeling a slight chill despite the rising temperatures of a scorching sun and a cloudless sky.

She was nearly ready, and the time was running down until she would be wed. It would be an enormous adjustment for her. In Nostria, she was viewed as part of a strong ruling house. Here, she would be an outsider, perhaps forever. Her smile had now vanished, replaced by a worried frown, and she suddenly felt the strains of the pressure on her to be nothing but beautiful but silent.

"What is it, Yami? What is wrong?" asked Joa with a concerned look.

But the Princess' eyes were somewhere far away, as if she had retreated to some place of solace inside her own soul. After a long minute, she finally replied.

"I don't think I am meant to be the Empress." she said.

~~~~~

The friends had wasted no time after landing the wasps outside of the entrance to Andoria's caverns, setting them free and hurrying inside to bring the Sword to the Chameleon King. It was morning, and the sun traced shadows of the canopy across the mossy forest floor as the companions raced into the cavern, tired and dirty.

The mystics all gathered to see the wonderful artifact, and Maxxus ordered that it be kept in the armouries, until a decision could be made about its fate. Once things settled, the friends were able to get cleaned up, rest, and share a good meal, which the chameleons prepared for them immediately. Chase ate little, and eventually went to find Maxxus again, in search of some answers for himself. The King was resting near the looking pool, but knew that the gecko had come with questions. He turned to speak with Chase, but was immediately distracted.

"Where did you get that knife?" asked The Chameleon King in astonishment, his orbital eyes both focused on the jewel-encrusted silver dagger.

Chase held it up a little higher for Maxxus to inspect, the question taking the gecko by surprise for a moment.

"We found it in the skeleton of a lizard deep in the rainforest, just before we found the Grove." Chase replied.

Maxxus almost gasped, but at the last second, he turned slightly away, even though one of his eyes lingered on the ornate blade. He was not able to hide his shock at seeing the weapon very well, and Chase's curiosity was immediately engaged.

"What is it? Obviously, you have seen this dagger before." said the gecko.

The King now turned completely away, stepping over to the looking pool in the rock.

"What else can you tell me about the remains of this reptile?"

Chase looked down at the dagger in his hands, paying more attention now to its carved silversides, and the gemstones carefully encrusted into its
~~~~~

hilt. It had light white rope binding the hilt as well, adding to the purity of its appearance. He remembered everything about when he and the others had found it. He recounted the scene for Maxxus.

"It was becoming dark by that time, and we were all tired. The rainforest growth finally turned from being the thick, trapping mess that we had fought through that day. Just as it cleared, we found a clearing, and that is where this skeleton was lying, with the dagger between its ribs. It had been there a long time, even some of the jungle vines were growing through its bones..."

As Chase finished speaking, he could see the Chameleon King lower his head slightly.

He cocked his head to one side, wondering what this was all about. Clearly, the dagger was made here in Andoria, and from the appearance of it, its construction was painstakingly detailed and lengthy work.

"What is it, my liege?" Chase asked. "What am I missing here?"

Maxxus remained silent for minutes, perhaps trying to script what he might say in his mind before speaking. There was little he could do but spill the words forth, and hope that it would all make sense to the young gecko. The sight of the dagger had pierced him as surely as if Chase had driven it into his flesh.

"If you explore your thoughts on this, then you might already know what I am about to tell you, my young friend..." said Maxxus.

Chase looked down at the dagger again, tracing its outline with his eyes. He thought about the clearing where they had found the reptilian skeleton.

The Chameleon King exhaled heavily.

"That dagger was a gift on the day of my coronation here in Andoria, the day I succeeded my father. I gave it to one of my dearest friends, a lizard whom I had known since we were both young. He had never failed us when the Great Wars came, and he and the militias drove the Stigians back time and again, despite the odds against them."

Chase listened intently, his mind lost in the scenes that Maxxus was describing.

"This lizard rescued the mountaintop Citadel of Nimisor, like you and your friends did." the King began again, turning to look upon the gecko. "He stole and hid the sword of Xanth from the Stigian Empire, ensuring that the Emperor could not send his troops across Evaria, invincible in their mission of conquest. It was only then that we could overcome the enemy, with all of our forces together. But the siege on Stigia had already failed, and the best we could do was force them to retreat back to the desert."

The young gecko's eyes were wide. He gazed up at the Chameleon King, his mouth open, but without words to speak. The sudden realization was stunning to him.

Maxxus could only nod to him, knowing that the impact of this knowledge would be hard on Chase.

"Even I was unable to see what happened that day, and if it weren't for the boasts from a certain Stigian Warlord, I would never have known what had become of my friend."

As Maxxus spoke, a single tear streamed down Chase's scales, and he gripped the hilt of the dagger tightly, bringing it close to his chest. His gaze dropped to the looking pool, as if he hoped to finally visualize what the King spoke of. As if he might see his father...

In the silence that followed his words, Maxxus watched the gecko's face, almost sorry he had said anything. As much as he felt the necessity to tell Chase the truth, it pained him to see the young gecko tormented by the sudden knowledge of what had happened. Some things were better off in the unknown, perhaps.

But now Chase at least knew what had become of his father, had learned that his father had made the ultimate sacrifice for what he believed in, for the protection of the realm. His deeds had been a well-known story, throughout all the races of Evaria.

Chase sank down onto the mosses of the grove, powerless to hold back the emotions he felt, combined with the realization of the identity of the remains they had found in the rainforest. His tears fell, unchecked, though he did not make a sound. Maxxus sat down beside him, resting a gloved hand on the gecko's shoulder.

"Your father was a hero to all in the realm. It is because of his actions that we do not live under Stigian rule right now. He was also a very good friend...You should be very proud of him, and the family name that you have carried on. You, yourself, have done great service to this world already." said the King solemnly.

Chase looked up at the Chameleon King, his eyes leaking tears as he replied.

"I am proud of who he was, and who I am. I wish I had been given more time with him is all..."

Chase stared off into space in the warmth of the cavern, and he could visualize his father's final battle with Cyrus Malthor…

~~~~~

The gecko knew who was coming toward him through the jungle undergrowth. Rasta had stopped running, catching his breath as he turned to finally face his pursuer. He could only hope that he had been able to lead them far enough away. It was daylight, and the Grove was once again camouflaged in normalcy. He no longer had the sword, but he still had his own silver blade. He stood in a large clearing, well away from where he had hidden the Sword of Xanth. It would be safe now, and the warlord and troops who were following him would not get their claws on it anytime soon.

Rasta could hear them crashing through the underbrush toward him, and knew that he would not be able to stay ahead of them. He had a wound on his right leg, a deep cut through his scales, just below the silver armour plate on his thigh. He had wrapped it crudely with a piece of his tunic to help stop the bleeding, but the pain had slowed him down quite a bit. There was no way he could outpace his pursuers.

As the noise of the Stigians grew louder, Rasta drew his sword slowly, remaining silent as his breathing slowed. This would be the end of running, regardless of what it cost him. He would make his stand here.

He had already completed his task, and now, the sword of power would not be found, the Emperor would not regain it and would have to abandon his campaign of conquest. He shuddered slightly to think of this warlord, Cyrus Malthor getting his claws on the sword. He had been relentless in his pursuit of Rasta and his militia, and insatiable for blood.

The growth at the edge of the clearing parted, and the dark scales and cruel eyes of the young warlord finally emerged into view. Several horned soldiers followed close behind Cyrus as he stepped clear of the tangling greenery, his cold gaze fixed on the gecko. The sight of Rasta with his sword drawn and ready caused the large lizard to raise an arm, motioning for the soldiers following him to stop. They obeyed, and an evil grin crept across the big uromastyx's face.

"So, the end has finally come for you and your pathetic forces, you will trouble the Stigian Empire no more, gecko!" Cyrus hissed gleefully. "Now tell me where the sword is, and I will make your death quick…"

Rasta smiled back at the warlord, raising his sword into the high guard.

"You going to need all those scum to fight me?" he asked sarcastically, his eyes flicking between Cyrus and the horned soldiers behind him.
~~~~~

Cyrus drew his long curved sword from its copper scabbard, the metal screaming.

"I don't need anyone to help me deal with the likes of you, little gecko!" he sneered, waving the soldiers off.

The two eyed each other carefully, despite the taunts. They had both been awaiting this moment for a very long time. Cyrus had wished to find this one gecko since the defeat of his forces attacking Nimisor, and Rasta knew that without this warlord, the Emperor's plans could never reach fruition. They hated one another.

Cyrus raised his sword, levelling it at Rasta, his eyes filling with hatred.

"This is your last day...I hope you have made your peace with that!" he said.

Rasta offered no reply, only giving his adversary a mocking grin, knowing that it would only serve to enrage his opponent further, increasing the possibility that he would make a fatal mistake.

"I beat you at the mountain Citadel, and your forces outnumbered us five to one…Hopefully, you can do better when we're one on one!" said Rasta.

This was the tipping point for Cyrus' emotions, and he charged the gecko with a cry of psychotic rage. He swung his sword blindly in a wide arc toward Rasta, the gecko parrying the attack and stepping aside neatly. Cyrus recovered quickly, turning back and attacking again. The sound of clashing steel filled the clearing, the horned soldiers watching the melee intently. The two combatants danced quickly around and toward one another as they traded blows.

Cyrus attacked the smaller gecko viciously, hammering the blade of his sword down onto Rasta's defensive maneuvers, even shoving him back at times if he could reach him during an attack.

The two reptiles paused suddenly, catching their breath. Rasta kept his sword in the high guard, ready for any treachery from the uromastyx as he tried to slow his breathing, his lungs on fire from the effort of the battle. He took advantage of the moment to further taunt Cyrus.

"Well, regardless of what happens here and now, your prize is lost to the secrets of the jungle. You will never have the Sword of Xanth again, nor will your master." he said.

Cyrus simply grinned evilly back at the gecko, not willing to give him the satisfaction of appearing angered any longer.

"You will die here today, gecko, and as far as the sword goes, I do not need a piece of ancient steel to bring this world to a knee before me. The Emperor's desire to recover that artifact is his ambition alone." hissed Cyrus, breathing heavily.

"You seem very sure of yourself. You are nothing but a puppet, and your strings are pulled by the Emperor. How does it feel to be a servant?" Rasta breathed, taking advantage of Cyrus' momentary pause.

The gecko's arrogant tone enflamed the Warlord's temper, and the uromastyx lunged forward angrily, bringing his sword down heavily upon his opponent's defending blade. He kicked viciously at the gecko, knocking him backwards to the floor of the clearing. Before Rasta could recover, he was upon him, pinning him down and placing his curved blade at his throat.

"You see now, how your insolent words do nothing but seal your fate?" said Cyrus, his eyes ablaze.

Rasta could not move, with the large reptile on top of him. He knew that he was finished, and that death was coming for him at any moment. Still, he looked up at Cyrus with defiance in his eyes. He still had the advantage in his own mind. No matter what might happen to him, he knew that the Sword would remain hidden. Without it, Evaria would not fall under the tyrannical rulership of Stigia.

"You have no real power, Cyrus…" said Rasta. "You are nothing."

The big lizard leered at the gecko, as he pulled something from Rasta's belt. It was a silver dagger, encrusted with gemstones, white ropes wrapping the hilt. He observed it briefly, grinning. His evil eyes turned back to the gecko, pinned beneath his sword blade.

"A gift from the mystics?" he sneered. "Perhaps the Chameleon King would look good with it stuck in his chest!"

"Talk all you like, Warlord. The rest of the realm will rise against your kingdom's oppression. Maxxus will kill your Emperor, and you, and leave both of you for the worms to feed on…"

The grin disappeared from Cyrus' scaled face, replaced by sheer rage. He plunged the dagger into the gecko's side, between the plates of his armour, twisting the blade cruelly. Rasta tried his best to hide the pain from his expression, as he fought to remain conscious.

"You will lose Cyrus, Stigia will lose…" he said weakly, his eyes becoming far away.

The Warlord twisted the blade once again, but the gecko refused to cry out. As life left him, he was content with the knowledge that he had not showed weakness, had remained strong in the face of his own end. He had triumphed, keeping the Sword of Xanth out of Stigian hands. Hopefully forever…

~~~~~

As the captain landed his wasp along with the other surviving reptiles of his troops, he could almost sense the dark cloud of his master's visage watching him. He could feel eyes upon him, boring into his flesh. And Aryan knew that the Emperor would not be happy with him returning empty handed. He had failed his Emperor, had failed his kingdom, and would have to pay the consequence. He would accept whatever fate his leader bestowed upon him. It was a decision he had made before ever landing back in Stigia.

Several horned soldiers rushed up to take hold of the wasp, leading it back toward the stables the moment the Captain had dismounted from it. The Captain wasted no time, flinging his cape aside, and stalking directly toward the keep. He knew what response to expect from his master, and his eyes remained icy and without emotion as he entered the cool of the shadows of the keep's halls. It struck him immediately, and he almost shivered with the sudden loss of the sun's heat.

The first thing that became noticeable was that the halls had been decorated for the Emperor's wedding, rare desert flowers were hung in clusters near the torch holders mounted along the sandstone walls. The polished onyx floors were spotlessly clean, and it was apparent that the servants had been kept very busy with preparations for the ceremony. It was a ceremony that the Captain was almost certain that he would likely not live to see. He would meet fulfill his destiny honourably, he promised himself. Whatever the results would be, he would accept them, even if it meant his very life.

He had no way of knowing that *The Three*, and their companions would have surprised them like they had, his troops had obviously not been trained well enough to react to such a situation. Had they been quicker, the group might not have escaped, and if they had the Sword, which he assumed they must, he would be presenting it to the Emperor right now.

But he accepted the fault as his, not theirs. Even if his leader chose to spare his life, the failure still would belong to him. As he took a turn down the hallways, climbing a sweeping staircase to the next floor of the keep, he tried to keep his thoughts in check. He would offer no excuses to the Emperor for his failure.

He approached the large wooden doors of the throne room, the two guards bowing properly to the Captain as he pushed the doors open and
~~~~~

entered. The Emperor was not on the throne, but seated at the map table over near the large window out onto the courtyard below. He did not look up as Aryan entered, gazing down at a map of the realm intently. There were also numerous servants scurrying about, placing tables and chairs, preparing decorations for the Emperor's wedding. Desert wildflowers were everywhere, a strange sight in the keep, where military and political matters usually trumped all else.

Aryan approached the table, bowing his head silently before his leader. He remained still and at attention, awaiting any response. Time seemed to drag on, and long minutes passed. The Captain began to become very uncomfortable, but remained still and obedient. Cyrus simply continued to study the map, shuffling a few parchments that he had made crude notes upon. Aryan dared not even clear his throat.

Eventually, the Emperor turned in his chair, pushing the papers aside abruptly. He glared at his Captain. Still, he said nothing. He rose slowly from his chair, stepping over to the window to observe the courtyard below, keeping his back to Aryan. He folded his scaled hands behind his back, his cape folding in tightly with the motion.

When Cyrus finally spoke, his voice bellowed through the throne room ominously.

"So, you have come back with nothing. And I understand that perhaps you let The Three get past your forces, and you do not have the Sword of Xanth?"

Aryan raised his head finally, grateful that the Emperor had finally engaged conversation with him. His voice was even and without fear as he replied.

"Yes, Your Grace. Sorry, Your Grace." was his simple response.

He chose not to describe the events that happened, how the rainforest was dark, lit only by their torches when the commotion of the giant centipede had erupted, how they had been surprised and overwhelmed by the sudden calamity. Aryan had also made a mistake in not having their wasps better guarded, which would have made it more difficult for The Three and their friends to escape.

The Emperor finally turned back toward him, stalking across to the table again. He drew his sword slowly, putting the point of its blade under the Captain's chin. His eyes blazed with anger. Failure was something that he despised. It was weakness. Despite all that Aryan had done in improving the troops skills, all that he had accomplished in better defenses for the city, Cyrus could not allow his commander to embarrass Stigia or him.

Aryan braced himself for the pain of his end, the agony that he knew would come when the Emperor decided to drive the blade through him. All he could hope was that it would be quick, that he would die a clean, honourable death. But the killing stroke did not come. The Captain remained rigid, every nerve on fire, although he allowed himself to show no emotion at all in the face of his certain execution.

"If not for the fact that the servants are already busy enough with their preparations for the ceremony to clean up more of a mess, I would kill you where you stand…" said Cyrus angrily.

"I accept full responsibility for failing you, Your Grace." replied Aryan quietly.

He was prepared to die, and waited to feel the sharp point of his master's steel enter his body. Instead, the blade lowered away from his chin. The Emperor returned it slowly to its scabbard, the steel making a metallic hiss as it slid out of view.

"Guards!" Cyrus shouted. "Arrest the Captain!"

Several of the Royal Guardsmen rushed over, their swords and spears pointed at their former commander. They stood in a defensive circle, surrounding him. Aryan did not move a muscle, and after a moment, he simply bowed his head again to the Emperor.

Cyrus paid little attention, motioning for the guards to take him into custody. They quickly stripped Aryan of his sword belt, roughly shackling his hands behind him. The Captain finally raised his eyes back to his leader, their icy stare intact, awaiting his judgment.

"Take him to the dungeon, he will await execution after the ceremony." hissed Cyrus, leaning in close to his Captain. "His death will be my bride's wedding gift…"

17

Alibesh stared at the tapestries in the armoury, her eyes lingering on the scenes depicting the Great War. It was something she had never seen before, battles that drew the entire realm into a confrontation with one another. The different races were all there in the paintings, working together to keep the desert Empire of Stigia from swallowing all of Evaria whole.

She traced her finger along the accompanying texts underneath the tapestries, reading about each part of the history that had been recorded about the fighting, about the death and destruction, about the thousands of lives that were lost on both sides of the conflict. The torchlight flickered across the painted fabric, and the etched parchments on display in the armoury, making shadows dance, seeming to bring the words and the scenes to life.

She was far too young for any memories of these times, having been born when the realm had begun a time of healing afterward. Few stories had been told in Sedda, as the skinks had elected not to become involved in the wars. She had only been taught of a time of great sorrow in her younger years. She remembered nothing of Andar, a few passing feelings if she smelled a particular scent, or heard the rain on the leaves of the rainforest was all she had. It was certainly not what these others she had come to know would feel about their home. Chase and Jonas, Kiko, even the big chameleon could identify a great deal more than she could with the forests here.

A pang of loneliness shot through her momentarily. These were *not* her friends. These were *not* her race. She was a reptile from the grasslands. *They* were her kind. She was a warrior, much more used to the brutality of combat than gathering berries or insects in the rainforests. But there was a sense of belonging here in Andoria that she could not shake off. It was a sense that she was meant to be here, with the others, amongst the gardens of the cavern. It was a beautiful place after all, and she had felt a sense of peace from the moment she had arrived. She was torn between returning home to the plains and remaining here amongst those of her own race. It confused her thoughts.

Tonight Alibesh felt clean and rested. The Chameleon mystics had provided her with some new clothing, modest but elegant, with soft fabric trimmed with colours as bright as the wildflowers growing in the gardens. The clothes were a little more girlish than she would have liked, and she probably would have felt more at home in armour, but it was nice to have been able to clean herself up. She returned her attention to the tapestries, trying to comprehend the entire image in front of her.

"It is a lot to take in, isn't it?" said a voice behind her.

It startled her, she was not used to being snuck up on, and she whirled around quickly, her arms raised in a defensive posture.

It was Chase. He immediately raised his hands in submission, with a guilty look on his face.

"Whoa. Sorry, I scared you." he said.

"Nothing scares me." She retorted hotly. "If I had my sword you might be dead now, actually."

Chase said nothing in return, just smiling softly at her. She relaxed quickly, turning her attention away from him. He had been very nice to her, which was something else she was not used to. And even though she had turned her eyes away from him, she had noticed that he too looked like he was cleaned up. His clothing had been cleaned, and he had shed the silver armour he and his friends had been wearing when they first met in the jungle. She pretended to be absorbed in the texts on the parchments on display once again.

"Where is your female anole friend tonight?" she asked, hoping to deflect any friendly approaches for the moment, but knowing at the last moment that the question would only serve to intrigue him.

"Kiko? She is enjoying a meal with Dantis and Jonas. Jonas is always hungry, if you haven't noticed." he said, nonplussed.

The female gecko held off on another response, preferring the silence she had been enjoying, accompanied by only the crackling of the torches in the large room. Other than saying something rude, she did not know how to make Chase disappear. And she wasn't sure that she really wanted to. He was nice to her, after all, despite her attempts to keep at a distance from his attention. Her thoughts continued to race, and she was unable to keep focused on the parchments or the tapestries.

"What is it you want?" she said finally, looking at him directly.

He just shrugged, with that smile still on his face. The smile agitated her. It disarmed her completely, and she hated that.

"I just didn't want you to feel like you were alone here." he said simply.

Alibesh's face flushed, and she hoped that it wasn't noticeable. She was not prepared for the way he was speaking to her. It was calm and kind. She was used to short and firm. And he had a look in his eyes that was starting to make her feel crazy. She just wanted to slap him. Almost.

She forced herself to turn back to the walls of the armoury, and she strolled away from him, looking at the weapons stored here as well. There were beautifully crafted weapons, swords and spears and shields, made of shining silver. Bows as well, made from the finest woods that the rainforests had to offer. And further down, the golden octagon encrusted with gemstones that had caught her attention upon first entering the room. The Gecko's Gate.

It had mesmerized her almost as much as the Sword of Power. The Sword stood here as well, as if to bring balance to that space of the stone wall. The radiance of the Gate, alongside the dark metal of the Sword of Xanth.

Alibesh's hands ached to hold the weapon once again. It was what she had sought her whole life, a perfectly crafted blade, stronger than any ever forged. It was perfect.

~~~~~

"So now what?" began Kiko. "Your Grace, you know that the Stigians will simply attack Andoria again. With both the Gate and the Sword here, it is almost a sure thing!"

She, Dantis and Jonas sat enjoying a wonderful meal which had been laid out for them by the chameleons, but the female anole's thoughts had been racing since they had arrived back at the cavern with the coveted ancient artifact. The Chameleon King had come to see them now that they were rested and cleaned up. Kiko had immediately begun a line of questions with the leader of the mystics. She simply did not understand the idea of going out to find the Sword, and bringing it to Andoria, where it could be the basis for the Emperor to make an attempt to take it by force.

"It won't be a guess on the part of Cyrus, his troops were surprised by us fleeing the Grove with it. I am sure at least some of them survived the centipede, and by now the Stigians all know it is here!" she continued.

Maxxus raised his hands patiently, waiting for her to finish her tirade. He smiled softly at her, knowing that it would do little to appease her questions and concerns.

"Please, my young friend…" he began slowly as she finished. "There is a plan in motion to protect these things, and the realm itself."

He tried to change the subject, seeing her tilt her head to him, obviously
~~~~~

not convinced. For the first time in an age, he had no answers for them, and was as sightless to the future as the rest of them.

"How is your dinner?" he pressed the companions.

Jonas could not physically answer, as his mouth was so full of food that all he could do was nod his head. Dantis chuckled watching him gorge himself on the meal in front of him.

"Just remember to breathe, Jonas." Maxxus said, grinning at the gecko.

The King looked around the area where the friends sat. The absence of two of the young reptiles immediately perked up his interest. They were usually all together, and he had only barely seen this female gecko from the grasslands when they had returned from their quest.

"Where is Chase?" he asked quickly.

Kiko's expression changed immediately, and Maxxus saw a different emotion fill her eyes for a moment. Jealousy.

"He's off entertaining his girlfriend." she said simply, pushing away from the table and stalking away without another word.

The King's orbital eyes switched between Dantis and Jonas, who only shrugged in response.

"When you two have finished eating, would you mind going to find Chase? I don't want him or this female gecko from Sedda to be out of our sight for very long."

Maxxus could not put his finger on it, but there was something out of place, and his looking pool had not been very forthcoming with any answers of late. He ignored the confused look from Dantis, turning to stroll back toward his grove and the pool in the rock. Even the beauty of the garden paths could not calm the unease he felt suddenly, and his thoughts took flight as he walked. The beauty of the cavern went unnoticed by his unfocused eyes, his mind preoccupied by the looming indecision he felt. He replayed what Kiko had said at the table when he had his approached, her words echoing in his brain. The young female anole was not wrong to be concerned about the treasures being both in Andoria at the same time. It was a delicate situation, one that could end very badly in the end. And where would the end bring them this time?

The King felt paralyzed without the flow of visions from his meditations by the pool. It was to be expected, he knew. The universe could not disclose all of its secrets to him, after all. As he reached the grove where the looking pool waited, he felt slightly more at ease. The best thing to do was to keep the companions altogether. To keep the artifacts safe. Time had flowed well beyond the Prophecy of The Three, and everything had become clouded in uncertainty. It was a time of great change in all of Evaria, that much Maxxus was certain of.

He entered the grove, settling down in his favourite comfortable place to meditate. But before he could relax totally, another mystic appeared through the trees surrounding his place of peace and silence. It was Ubius. The King greeted him with a pleasant smile and a nod.

"My friend. What news?" Maxxus said.

"There is no movement of Stigian troops nearby, according to our scouts, Your Grace. But I don't think it will be long before that will change." he replied.

"If the Emperor of the desert kingdom has received word that the Sword has been found, it is indeed a dangerous time." said the King.

"Yes, especially if he knows it is here, alongside the Gecko's Gate." said Ubius.

The Chameleon King explored his options, trying to decide what was best for his kingdom. Not only Andoria, but the rest of the realm as well. Kiko was young, but her interpretation of what would likely come was right. As was Ubius'. It was time to make a decision, and Maxxus knew that they must make themselves ready for the anger of the Stigian Emperor. As he spoke slowly, the old chameleon's voice took on a grim undertone.

"I think you are probably correct, Ubius… Let's speed word to the other leaders of what has transpired here. Perhaps I will require my armour once more. Ready our forces for an assault."

<div align="center">~~~~~</div>

The sun was high in the desert sky as Cyrus was being dressed by the servants for his wedding. He ignored them, his gaze remaining out the window, watching the courtyard, and the arid expanse of the Sand Sea beyond. He could imagine his empire stretching from sea to sea, encompassing the whole of Evaria. To conquer all of the world would complete a campaign that no other Emperor before him had been able to do. He was so close to achieving it, despite the frustration of letting the Sword of Xanth slip through his fingers. His thoughts turned to his nemesis, the Chameleon King. He would crush him, along with the other chameleon mystics, and take the sword back by force. As soon as his plans here in Stigia were finished, once he had control of the badlands and its assassins, he would launch a force toward the races of the rainforest that had never been seen before in the history of the realm.

Aryan had failed him, but he would find a new commander for the armies, and another again if this one failed him. He would hang them from the walls of the city until he found a reptile that would succeed in bringing him victory and conquest. Perhaps another of the monitors would be found that was ruthless and precise enough to lead his troops on the battlefields that awaited.

For the moment, he had to focus on the present, had to proceed with wedding the Princess of Nostria. He would then dispose of the Lord, Taran, and with his bride beside him, he would declare the north to be a part of the Empire. Any who resisted would meet a quick end, and he would have the grandest army of any that had ever called Stigia home.

Vitos appeared through the doors of the Emperor's chambers.

"Your Grace. It is time. The throne room awaits your arrival for the wedding ceremony." he said.

Cyrus turned, shooing away the servants.

"Very Well. Is everything in place for my plans?" he asked.

"Yes, Emperor…" Vitos replied.

The old lizard had arranged a plan to have the refreshments in the rooms for Taran poisoned after the ceremony, ridding Cyrus of the Lord of Nostria, and making room for the Emperor's plans involving the north. It was a plan worthy of the assassins themselves.

Cyrus grinned evilly at the short horned lizard, sweeping his cape behind him and stalking toward the doors, Vitos and his guards following quickly behind. They proceeded down the sandstone hallways, the onyx floors polished to a mirror shine, reflecting the torchlight. Desert wildflowers and ribbon lined the fixtures in the hallways of the keep, and a great celebration had been organized for the city to follow the ceremony. None of this mattered to Cyrus, however. The Emperor spoke not a word as they neared the throne room, the royal guards posted outside pulling open the huge wooden doors obediently.

The entourage entered the room, where hundreds of horned lizards both citizens and soldiers were gathered. Lush red carpeting led the Emperor to the raised platform where his throne awaited, along with another smaller version, which was not quite as ornate, but made of the same black wood as the throne itself. It was for his bride, who would become the Empress of Stigia.

Every eye in the room was on him as he strode down the carpeted walkway, and up to the throne, his guards taking their positions close by, and

Vitos standing to the side of the raised platform, his scaled hands folded in front of him. He would preside over the wedding, as one of the duties of the office he held in the city. This was the first time since the first Emperor of Stigia that a leader had actually been wed, and the first time Vitos would carry out the task.

Cyrus turned toward the crowd of onlookers, and the entire room bowed to their Emperor. He revelled in their undivided attention. Horns sounded to announce the arrival of his bride. All of the masses gathered in the throne room turned to see their new Empress enter.

18

The female gecko turned her eyes toward Chase, and he saw something strange there suddenly. She had a look that he had only seen when they first met in the darkness of the rainforest. It unsettled him, but his blood felt hot flowing through his veins. She had a strange grip on him, one that he could not identify. He loved her dark, shining scales, her large, vertically slit eyes. She was beautiful to him. For a moment, he felt a pang of shame again. What would Kiko think if she could read his thoughts? He turned his eyes away for a moment, knowing he was blushing slightly.

"What is it?" he asked, trying not to appear shaken.

She glanced back to the wall where the Gecko's Gate, and the Sword were displayed.

"How does it work? It is beautiful." she asked, gesturing toward the golden octagon.

The male gecko paused for a moment, thinking back to all that he, Jonas, and Kiko had been through, the quests, the prophecy. It had been a long road already, and he did not consider himself old by any means. They were all still quite young and had been from one end of the realm to the other, it seemed. They bore the scars of several battles already, and there was no real end in sight to the threats to their world.

Chase recounted the tale of when they had used it to trick Cyrus at Nimisor, trapping him in the ice fields to the south. He almost had trouble remembering all the details, it had seemed so long ago.

Alibesh listened intently to all of his story, her eyes glistening in the fire light of the torches in the armouries. He became lost in them as he spoke, telling her all about how they had used the gate to save the realm from Cyrus, before he had returned and taken the throne of Stigia as Emperor. He told her of the battles since then, the assassins and how they had saved the Chameleon King from certain death. He told her of serpents and seas. She was enthralled with his words, and he continued for a long time. When he finally finished, she looked like a hatchling listening to one of Lanwyn's stories back in Andar in the Great Hall.

She sighed deeply, gazing back at the golden artifact hanging on the wall.

"So it can only take you to a place you have seen before?" she asked in amazement.

Chase nodded, looking up at it as well, and the dark metal of the Sword of Xanth hanging next to it. The smooth gold surface of the jewel-encrusted octagon shone brilliantly in the light of the torches of the armouries, its ancient metal radiant and perfect.

She suddenly looked back at him, her eyes wide and bright.

"So let's use it! Let's go to Stigia and destroy the Emperor, we could use the sword against him!" she exclaimed.

Chase exhaled deeply. And then he let out a chuckle.

"I would love to do that, but I think it would be best to let Maxxus decide what we should do first." he replied.

She shrugged her shoulders at him in exasperation.

"Why? You and I could kill Cyrus Malthor, and rule all of the realm eventually. We could bring about peace!" said Alibesh.

Chase turned, thinking about all that she was saying. It had never occurred to him that they could do that, especially on their own without the counsel of the Chameleon King, or anyone else for that matter. It would also mean leaving his home in Andar, and his friends. At least for a while. The flood of ideas that Alibesh was suggesting was dizzying, and he took a minute to think about all of it. He did not like the idea of doing something rash without at least speaking to Maxxus first.

"I don't think that is a good —"

His words were cut short as he was struck suddenly on the head from behind, his legs giving way beneath him, and his vision becoming foggy as unconsciousness began to take over. Alibesh stood over him, with the Sword of Xanth in her hand hilt first. She had struck him with it hard, and as his eyes closed, she grabbed the golden octagon from the wall above. She looked down on him in disappointment as his eyes began to roll. She did not wish to hurt him, but she would also not allow him to stand in the way of her plans.

"Too bad, Chase. We could have had everything, together..." she said, activating the Gate.

~~~~~

Yami entered the throne room, the young female monitor's face covered
~~~~~

in transparent white silk, her gown flowing behind her as the horns continued to sound. Her heart beat heavily in her chest. There were too many reptiles present. The entire throne room was full, and each one of them had their eyes on her. She tried to maintain focus, putting one foot in front of the other to reach the spot that she was supposed to be in front of the raised platform of the throne. The last thing she wanted was to fumble, or stumble, and embarrass herself in front of this throng.

Her father was ahead, near the platform, and she concentrated on him. He stood proudly watching her approach, a soft smile on his face. She could not bear the thought of disappointing him, and tried her best to return his smile. She took her time, being careful that her gown did not catch her feet, standing straight and tall as she moved forward. Yokady, Maily, and Joa followed behind, dressed in short white gowns as well, although much more muted than the Princess' attire. They reached the end of the walkway, where a large pillow had been set out. Yami knelt down, sitting on the comforting velvet, keeping her bouquet held up in front of her chest. Her three friends knelt on the carpet behind her. The horns sounded loudly one last time, and the guards at each of the columns in the throne room thumped the butt of their spears against the polished floor in unison. The ceremony would begin. All gathered in the throne room went quiet, watching intently as the scene began to unfold.

Vitos stepped forward, opening a small scroll to read from. He was regally dressed in robes which foretold his position, ones which he wore only for ceremonies of such importance as the one he was presiding over on this day.

"Those gathered here in the city and Empire of Sigia behold!" he began, his old voice echoing in the now silent room. "We gather here to witness the union of our beloved Emperor, Cyrus Malthor, to the beautiful Princess Yami of Nostria on this day in the realm of Evaria!"

Applause burst forth briefly from those gathered in the throne room.

Yami refused to look at the Emperor, crouched on her pillow in the middle of the red carpet, below the raised platform where Cyrus stood. She knew now that this was not going to play out well for her in any way. Her father stood close by, and Maily, Yokady, and Joa were knelt directly behind her. It brought no comfort to her. She would be a prisoner here in Stigia, and little more.

The Empire was just a seething, arid place of hatred for the rest of Evaria, and the Princess knew that from this day forward, she would be remembered only as a piece of the murderous and evil faction that ruled the desert kingdom. There would be no peace here. And she would not be free to enable the citizens of Stigia to have a better life in the future.

Vitos continued to speak, making his way through the words that would forever bind her to the Empire, and to the Emperor's side. She glanced up at the uromastyx who stood tall above her. He smiled an evil smile as he looked out upon the room, and the reptiles gathered for the ceremony. She hated the thought of being here any longer, wishing that she was at home, watching the tumbleweeds blown across the arid steppes of the badlands.

A brilliant flash of blue light suddenly erupted in front of her, at the base of the platform where Cyrus was standing. It was blinding, momentarily causing all nearby to shield their eyes. On the floor, she could just make out a glowing golden octagon, the light growing up out of it. The light diminished slightly after a few seconds, still there, but not as intense. Yami looked upward, seeing a figure standing directly in front of her with its back to her. The princess squinted despite the veil of silk covering her face, trying to see more. It was a female form, dressed in a simple dress, with a large black blade held in both hands. She was a gecko. She was facing the Emperor, who also had shielded his eyes from the blinding light.

Before any of the guards in the throne room could have hoped to react, the female gecko thrust the black sword blade directly into the Emperor's chest, screaming a primal war cry. Her hands were strong and steady, her mission clear in her mind. She thrust the blade further into his flesh, ensuring her kill. Blood flowed from the wound, as Cyrus screamed in pain, grabbing the blade as he fought to maintain his balance.

The shocked citizens of Stigia gasped, and panic quickly gripped the crowd, turning the ceremony into a chaotic stampede of reptiles seeking nothing but escape from the horrific scene.

The Emperor fell to his knees, unable to overcome the strength of this female attacker, as dark reptilian blood pooled around him on the polished floors of the throne room. His life was over, and despite his attempts to pull the blade from his flesh, he sank further down as the gecko locked eyes with him, her own filled with no emotion. She remembered her treatment here in the desert kingdom, remembered the death sentence that this uromastyx had tried to hand down to her in the arena. Regret would be the last thing she felt at this time.

As the residents of the city fled the room, Yami saw a brief window of opportunity. She turned quickly toward her female companions, motioning for them to follow her as she lunged forward. They moved forward with her without question. The princess reached out, grabbing hold of the scaled arm of her astonished father, dragging him into the portal of light with them. They disappeared into the radiant blue light, vanishing into thin air as the melee continued.

Alibesh spun part way around, seeing the monitors dive toward the light of the Gate. She let it happen, maintaining her grip on the Sword of Power with both hands as the Emperor writhed in pain, dying in front of her. She did not care about the notion of escape at this point. Finishing what she had come here to do was the only thought in her mind.

Cyrus glared at her, unable to speak, but his eyes told Alibesh how much he hated her right at the moment. He raised a clawed hand toward her, feebly trying to grasp for her. His eyes were filled with hatred, even as they began to fade. His hand fell powerlessly to his side as he finally slunk to the floor, the blood still flowing from his mortal wound. His body went still at last.

Alibesh exhaled slowly, feeling the calm after the kill entering her body. She yanked the sword free of the Emperor's corpse, spinning around with it held high to confront any reptile that might be foolishly coming toward her. But there was nothing. The guards stood with open mouths at the entire scene, Vitos cowering on the floor nearby.

The light from the Gate suddenly disappeared within the golden octagon, it too vanishing from sight. She was trapped here. They had closed the Gecko's Gate from the other side. The thought registered, but she felt no fear or remorse. She had accomplished what she had set out to do. Cyrus was dead. The Emperor was no more.

She maintained her defensive posture even now that the throne room was mostly silent, the remaining onlookers having fled the throne room. She knew that the guards were no match for her, but there were a considerable number of them, and she could be overwhelmed by them if they charged at once. But instead of attacking her, the guards did something quite different than what she was expecting. One by one, they took a knee before her. Setting their spears and swords on the floor, they lowered their heads to her in reverence. Vitos finally recovered as well, bowing to her deeply. She stayed in her defense, a confused look on her face.

"My lady, you have killed the Emperor of Stigia. It is to you, now, that we must pledge ourselves to…" said Vitos. "You are now the one who must rule our kingdom, without question. It is our law."

She slowly relaxed, keeping vigilant but lowering the sword. Her look of confusion was slowly replaced by a small smirk, as she realized what the old horned lizard was saying.

"Please, Your Grace. We await your orders…" urged the old horned lizard.

~~~~~

Maxxus could not believe what he was seeing in the looking pool now that it had finally cleared. His meditation abruptly ended, he staggered to his feet in disbelief, leaving the grove where he had his visions at once in the direction of the armouries. Ubius joined him, seeing the obvious concern on the King's face as they rushed across the cavern toward the stone building which housed the Gecko's Gate and the Sword of Xanth.

Kiko spotted them from one of the gardens of wildflowers next to the stream, and immediately knew that something had happened. Shouting to Jonas and Dantis, she sped off to join the Chameleon King. Her immediate thoughts went straight to Chase, as she did not see him anywhere, and the haste made by Maxxus and Ubius made her heart race that something bad was going on. She felt a slight panic, running in a flat out sprint, without waiting for the others. What would she do if something had happened to Chase? A million thoughts raced through her mind as she ran. She flashed back to late night walks with him in the rainforest, to leisurely swims in the river. She remembered the way he would look at her in the Great Hall during Lanwyn's story times when he thought she didn't notice. Whatever was going on, it had to be something to do with that female gecko, Alibesh. Kiko hated her. She could not put her finger on it, but she did not trust her at all, there was something there behind her eyes that sent warning bells to Kiko.

As they all arrived at the armouries together, Kiko darted up the stone steps, suddenly realizing that she had no weapon in hand. It didn't matter. If Alibesh had done anything to harm Chase, she would kill her with her bare hands.

Maxxus and the others followed behind, Jonas and Dantis bringing up the rear. What met their eyes as they turned the corner was both unexpected, and amazing. A young female monitor, along with three others, and an older, wrinkled male stood at the far end of the room, as Chase struggled to get up from the floor, holding his aching head. The female monitors gasped slightly in surprise at the sight of the group entering the room. The one female was
~~~~~

holding the Gecko's Gate, and slowly placed it on the floor in front of her, stepping back carefully. Her face was covered in a veil, obscuring her face. Maxxus' orbital eyes darted amongst them, shocked at what he was seeing.

Chase staggered back away from the monitors, confused. Kiko and Jonas rushed forward, steadying him. Chameleon guards ran into the room behind the group, swords drawn. Maxxus immediately held a hand to them to stop where they were. The monitor dressed in the gown reached quickly for a spear hanging close by on the wall to defend herself and her companions.

The Chameleon King raised his arms to them, indicating that there was no danger to them, that all was well.

"If you look around you, you will see no enemies here…" said Maxxus. "Welcome to Andoria."

"A-Andoria?" replied the monitor "Is that where we are?"

"Yes, you have travelled through the Gecko's Gate it would appear. You are from Nostria, are you not?" asked Maxxus.

The young monitor relaxed the spear, and removed the veil covering her face, tossing it to the floor.

"Yes, I am the Princess, Yami, and this is my father, the Lord of Nostria, and master of the guilds. We were-"

"You were in Stigia." finished Maxxus. "And what became of the gecko, Alibesh?"

Chase rubbed his head again.

"She took the Sword of Xanth, and used the Gate to go to Stigia to try to kill Cyrus." he said groggily.

"And she succeeded." stated Yami bluntly. "We used the Gate to escape here. I believe that they were going to kill us, and take over Nostria without being challenged."

"Cyrus is dead?!?" asked Chase and Kiko in unison.

"Yes." replied Maxxus. "I have seen it in my visions. But I fear he has only been replaced by a far more evil leader. Alibesh does not go to Stigia to stop evil, but to give it a different face. Now that she has the Sword with her, she will not be easily stopped."

~~~~~

Alibesh took her place on the throne of Stigia, dressed in glistening black armour, and a cape as red as blood. The Sword of Power hung at her side, its dark metal giving forth no shine in the light of the torches. An entire legion knelt before her, along with a unit of assassins from Nostria, those who had
~~~~~

been caught up in this strange situation.

As she looked out over the reptiles in front of her, she could not help but let a smile creep onto her face. They would gladly die for her. It was the first time she had felt this kind of power over anyone or anything. She liked it very much. She would sculpt this Empire into her own creation, re-make it to her own liking.

She had already ordered the copper colours of her troops be shed in favour of black and red. The armouries were already being changed, the monuments to past Emperors dragged down and destroyed. Cyrus' own sandstone statue was in the midst of being disassembled. The female gecko hated that type of vanity, and sought to immediately erase Cyrus from the histories of Stigia.

Vitos appeared before the throne, bowing deeply to Alibesh. She had kept him in his position, respecting his knowledge of protocol and the histories of Stigia.

"Your Grace, what are your orders?" he asked.

She thought for long minutes, considering all that had happened. Standing up from the black wood of the throne, she strode coolly over to the large window out on the courtyard. The sun was sinking low over the Sand Sea, making the shadows long, the cool of the coming night riding on the desert breeze. Her eyes lingered over everything, the cobblestone yard below, the guards manning the city walls. Her city. Her Empire.

"Your briefing said that the Captain of the armies remains imprisoned in the dungeons?" she said to Vitos absently.

The short, old lizard stepped forward to her side quickly.

"Yes, Your Grace. Do you wish to go ahead with his execution?" he asked.

Alibesh turned away from the window stepping back to her throne, Vitos following on her heels. She sat back down, running her hands over the heavy black wood.

"No. Have him released. And tell him to report to me immediately." she finally responded.

He bowed to her, an incredulous look on his wrinkled face. He turned, snapping his fingers at two nearby guards, who turned to leave, carrying out the orders.

Later, her quarters were prepared, in a different room of the keep than her predecessor had occupied. Vitos also toured Alibesh through the rest of the important places of the city. She stayed for a while in the libraries, reading some of the Empire's historical papers. She was brought a great meal, which she ate back in the throne room, now that it was empty, except for her royal guards, now dressed in her preference of black armour. She sat eating silently, contemplating the many changes she would make to her new world. She ate at the map table, close to the window where the draperies where stirred by the breeze. The sun set over the desert, and the torches were lit to illuminate the room by several servants.

As they exited the throne room, the guards escorted another horned lizard in, his eyes icy and devoid of feeling. He stood in the middle of the room and bowed to Alibesh politely as the guards stood back.

Alibesh turned toward him, pushing her plate away.

"You are Aryan, the Commander of the armies?" she asked.

"I was, Your Grace." he replied.

She stood up from the table, walking slowly toward him, her red cape sweeping along the polished floor. She stopped a few feet in front of him, her eyes tracing over him intently. He remained still and silent.

"I don't recall relieving you of duty, and I am the one who rules this Empire now, luckily for you." she said, a slight grin emerging on her face as she began to walk slowly again, circling him.

"Stigia seems to be a place where the soldiers follow their master's orders, no matter what may become of them. Do you follow in this belief?" she asked.

"Yes, Your Grace." he replied firmly, his eyes staring forward.

"And will you defend me at all costs, prepared to sacrifice you own life if necessary, Captain?" she purred, continuing her stroll around him.

"I will." he stated simply.

The torches in the throne room flickered, as though applauding Aryan's affirmation. Alibesh withdrew the Sword of Power from her side, holding its point at the commander's neck.

"And you are willing to pay the ultimate price for any further failure?" she asked.

Pushing the limits of their cordial conversation suddenly, the Captain retorted fairly harshly.

"I do believe my recent failure also allowed Your Grace to escape and live!"

Alibesh looked into Aryan's icy eyes, her grin growing wider.

"You are correct, which is why I should kill you right here and now!" she said.

For a moment, Aryan thought that she might kill him indeed. But she lowered the sword, replacing it at her side. She stalked back up onto the platform, lounging back into the throne. She watched him for long minutes.

"Will you swear to bring me victory on the battlefield, following any order without question?" She finally asked.

The Captain took a knee before her, lowering his head solemnly.

"I will. I swear it, Empress!"

ABOUT THE AUTHOR

Dennis Stein lives in Ontario, Canada, in a small city next to the Thousand Islands. He only began to take writing seriously in 2010, and has written a number of titles, across multiple genres since.

He first visited the world he created in 2005, putting together the basis for the epic story of the far off world of Evaria, a ringed planet around a single sun, where evolution went on a very different path from our own planet. The story has lived in his mind since, a place that he continually sculpts and brings his readers further into with each new installment to the series.

The Empress opens up all new drama in the realm, adding new characters and exciting new settings in the ever expanding universe of the Gecko's Gate. This third tale brings an all new storyline to the saga, in a title that Stein promises will not be the last in the series. One can only wonder what might come next…